INDIAN GIVING

At first Skye Fargo was grateful to the Indian captors who had given him a sip of water. But now his gratitude was fading fast as he saw the stones that the Indians had put into the fire becoming white hot.

The medicine man, Yellow Dog, smiled. "You thought we were being compassionate, white man," he said. "All we did was prolong your pain. Your suffering will begin when the stones are so hot we can see through them."

"And when will that be?" Fargo asked.

"One more moon and you will not see the new day. Nobody will kill you. You will kill yourself. . . ."

THE TRAILSMAN 96

BUZZARD'S GAP

by

Jon Sharpe

A SIGNET BOOK

NEW AMERICAN LIBRARY

A DIVISION OF PENGUIN BOOKS USA INC.

PUBLISHER'S NOTE

This is a work of fiction. Names, characters, places, and incidents either are the product of the author's imagination or are used fictitiously, and any resemblance to actual persons, living or dead, events, or locales is entirely coincidental.

The first chapter of this book previously appeared in *Cry Revenge*, the ninety-fifth volume in this series.

SIGNET TRADEMARK REG. U.S. PAT. OFF. AND FOREIGN COUNTRIES
REGISTERED TRADEMARK—MARCA REGISTRADA
HECHO EN DRESDEN, TN, U.S.A.

SIGNET, SIGNET CLASSIC, MENTOR, ONYX, PLUME, MERIDIAN
and NAL BOOKS are published by New American Library, a division of
Penguin Books USA Inc., 1633 Broadway, New York, New York 10019

First Printing, December, 1989

1 2 3 4 5 6 7 8 9

PRINTED IN THE UNITED STATES OF AMERICA

The Trailsman

Beginnings . . . they bend the tree and they mark the man. Skye Fargo was born when he was eighteen. Terror was his midwife, vengeance his first cry. Killing spawned Skye Fargo, ruthless, cold-blooded murder. Out of the acrid smoke of gunpowder still hanging in the air, he rose, cried out a promise never forgotten.

The Trailsman, they began to call him, all across the West: searcher, scout, hunter, the man who could see where others only looked, his skills for hire but not his soul, the man who lived each day to the fullest, yet trailed each tomorrow. Skye Fargo, the Trailsman, the seeker who could take the wildness of a land and the wanting of a woman and make them his own.

*June, 1860, on the baking plains
of Nebraska Territory, where the lure
of the promised land to the West
was almost as strong as
the hand of Death . . .*

1

A scorching sun high in the chalky sky beat down fiercely on the big man astride the black-and-white Ovaro. He rode in unusually still air where not even rattlers moved in the blistering heat. He'd never known the Great Plains area to be this hot before, and he wondered if the broiling summer would be worthy enough for the Sioux to record in their winter count.

Streams of heat waves rippled from the ground and hung murderously, undulating for fifty feet or more above the parched and cracked Nebraska landscape. They acted like an imperfect magnifying glass that made landmarks appear distorted and closer than they actually were.

Sweat ran down his muscled back as he looked toward the western horizon for signs that promised rain. A lone thunderhead building in the far distance would do, or a distinct black arc heralding an onrushing summer storm. He saw nothing but an endless searing sky void of anything save the torturous heat.

The big man adjusted his neckerchief higher on the bridge of his nose, wiped sweat from his brow with a finger, then squinted his lake-blue eyes to see better through the silent movement of energy. His gaze swept the jagged outline of a barrier wall of rock. He knew the barren formation ran more or less north and south for miles in both directions. A traveler going this way had only two options: lose a day or two going around one end, or focus on the misshapen twin spires of rock that rose out of the barrier at its center. The latter choice offered the shortest route and the least resistance. It was also the most dangerous. The Trailsman rode straight for the two peaks.

They stood towerlike, separated by little more than a wagon's width. Like the rest of the long obstacle, the lofty turret's outer surfaces angled down and away sharply, making passage impractical except through the narrow slot.

Before him and slightly to the left stood a lone boulder polished smooth by millennia of blowing sand and rain. The enormous stone seemed to be growing out of the ground about halfway between him and the narrow opening.

Well above the two peaks a shimmering dark cloud of buzzards circled slowly. Their flight on such a hot day in this desolate stretch of rolling plains foretold danger.

Fargo thought he glimpsed movement. Now that he looked closely, he saw Indian ponies in the gap. The Indians were on the ground, ransacking overturned wagons. He angled the pinto to put the boulder directly between him and the movement.

At the boulder he halted to peer around it through the dense heat. The Indians, a small war party, no more than eight or ten, had obviously waited for the wagons—he counted five: two Owensboros modified for canvas cover tops and three Conestogas—to clear the slot before attacking from this side. The Indians' unhurried activity told the Trailsman all of the settlers had been killed.

As he watched, a shot was fired. The bullet glanced off the stone, whined off in the heat. The big man withdrew his Sharps from its saddle case, brought the butt of the stock to his left shoulder, aimed at a brave, and squeezed off a round. The impact knocked the man backward. The others quickly mounted their ponies and charged for the boulder.

Skye Fargo leveled his sights on the lead rider, shot him off the pony, moved onto another redskin, and blew him to the ground. The others wheeled and raced back for the wagons.

Fargo emptied the Sharps as he chased after them, shooting two more off their mounts. He returned the Sharps to the saddle case and drew his big Colt. The Indians regrouped behind the wagons and began firing at him. Bullets whizzed past his face as he charged in. Sliding from the saddle, he shot two point-blank in the head. The remaining savages—he now saw they were Omahas—tried to disengage and make a run for it.

Fargo stepped boldly in their path and blasted another pair from their ponies. The sole survivor dived from his mount with a club poised to slam into Fargo's skull. He sidestepped the oncoming war club and hurtling Omaha, turned, and waited for him to stop tumbling. When the Indian rose, Fargo blew an angry red hunk of painted flesh out of the man's face.

Holstering the Colt, he glanced around the ground littered with bodies. He counted sixteen settlers—six men, five women, and five youngsters. The women and three of the youngsters, all girls, were naked and, like all the others, scalped. He could only imagine the females' terror as the renegade Omahas, almost as fierce as the

Sioux just north of here, went about their sordid deeds before favoring them with death.

Fargo slid from the saddle, then searched through the debris until he found a serviceable pick and shovel.

By sunset he'd buried the settlers' remains in a common grave in the shadows of the sheer rocky rises a short distance from the gap. He tossed the digging tools on the mound of earth and left them as a marker, a grim reminder for all to see and remember; death lurks in tight places that lead only one way. Dusting off his hands, he looked down at the grave, then spoke in an almost reverent whisper. "At least you're out of the baking sun."

He whistled the big Ovaro to him. While the pinto came, the big man cut his eyes to the dead Indians, then up to the buzzards watching from their lofty perches on the twin spires. "Dinner's ready," he hissed. He put one boot in the stirrup, swung up onto the saddle, and rode through the gap.

On the western side he moved into the gigantic fiery red arc of sun. A stand of lodgepole pine and bur oak with red willow hugged the banks of a creek-fed pond within a mile of the massacre site. There he built a small cooking fire, fixed a trail meal, and brewed the last of his coffee. He drank it from a tin cup while staring deep in thought at the glowing embers.

Again he wondered about the magnetic force of the West. How it could pull so many people toward it so easily when they all realized the ever-present danger it held. Again he concluded they were drawn to it for much the same reasons as he had been, its natural beauty and the total freedom it offered. The danger and risk weren't enough to stop them from pulling up stakes to go west.

Sighing, Fargo reached over and fetched his bedroll, then spread it on the still-warm ground. He undressed and lay down to gaze at the inky sky while drifting into sleep. He fell asleep glancing among stars and constellations long familiar to him, not unlike lighthouses that show seamen their way along treacherous coasts at night.

Fargo awoke at first light. He set the old coffee grounds to boil again while he saddled the pinto, then he went to the pond to wash up and fill his canteen. He took two sips of the strong brew, then tossed the rest away. After he'd sloshed the cup and pot in the stream, he packed them away, then mounted up and rode away with his back to the rising sun.

Just before sundown, he arrived on a boulder-strewn ridge that overlooked a one-street town far below. A creek coursed along the base of the sheer rocky wall. On the other side of the stream was a hamlet of six structures, three on each side of the wide sunbaked street. One structure, he noted, had two levels. A balcony fronted the building, which he decided was a saloon with upstairs living quarters. The weatherbeaten wood siding had never seen a drop of paint.

To the south of the little town stood a white church. Near it were two parked covered wagons that seemed to be modified Owensboros. A group of six people stood at the rear of one of the wagons.

Then he saw them. They rode in with their backs to the setting sun: five eerie red-rimmed silhouettes coming hard, straight out of the huge, fiery red-orange arc, as if fleeing hell.

Fargo glanced at the Ovaro grazing on a clump of prairie grass. Looking back at the horsemen, Buzzard's Gap flashed to mind. Maybe they were coming to warn the town that the Omaha were on the warpath again.

He watched the group enter the hamlet from its northern end, expecting to see townsfolk gather quickly. Instead, they scattered. The new arrivals started whooping and shooting in all directions. Windowpanes in shops shattered, slugs slammed, crunched into wood. A near-spent round buzzed past Fargo's chiseled face and ricocheted off the boulder behind the pinto, startling the magnificent animal.

This band of riders hadn't come to warn anyone about anything, or even to have an evening of drinking and fun. Only to bring trouble. Of its own accord, his massive right hand went to the handle of his holstered Colt.

"Easy, boy," he told the Ovaro as he continued to observe the developing scene down below.

Two of the horsemen—one tall, the other short and astride a big dun—rode inside the two-story structure, firing as they entered. Fargo heard a female screaming amid their gunfire. More glass broke, and even from this great distance he heard furniture overturn.

The other three dismounted and ran in different directions. One started breaking into businesses already closed for the day, while another ran toward the wagons by the church. When the startled people saw him, they broke and ran for safety inside the white building, but he shot all of them before any could make it. Then he moved among the fallen people, shooting each person in the head. Fargo saw the man tilt his head back and heard his distant, hollow laugh. The killer fired two more bullets into women's bodies before going back to join his shaggy-haired partner in the street. He yelled to those in the saloon, "Chase a few out for me an' Luke. Send us the big uns, Paw."

Four men gripping handguns came out, two through windows on the balcony. The other two crashed through the saloon's lower front windows. Before any could get up and shoot, the two men in the street shot them dead, then hollered for more. Fargo noticed the female's screaming had ceased.

As he moved back toward the Ovaro, an explosion

stopped him in midstride. Out of reflex he turned, the big Colt poised to fire, then holstered the gun as he stepped back to the rim of the ridge. Looking down, he saw a building across from the saloon had been blown to smithereens. What little of it remained was all ablaze.

He turned his back on the grisly scene. Three strides put him to the Ovaro. Grim-jawed, Fargo grasped the saddle horn, poked his left boot in the stirrup, and swung up into the saddle. Reining the pinto around the boulder, he glanced at the fresh nick left on it by the stray bullet, and mumbled, "That one had my name on it, and it damn near got me. Some fool's going to die."

Darkness consumed the ridge as the Trailsman negotiated the Ovaro down through the boulder-strewn far side, then through the tight cut that led down to the devastated hamlet, Gully Town.

Passing the church, he saw the marauders fleeing north from the razed town. He spurred the Ovaro after them. He emptied the Colt into the vanishing pack and heard one of them shriek he'd been hit. He lost sight of them when they divided and disappeared into the black night.

Fargo rode back to Gully Town and surveyed the murderers' wanton harvest of death and destruction. Seven corpses lay askew in muddy puddles of their own blood in the street. The remains of one wall of the building the gang had blown up continued to burn. As he watched, this entire section collapsed inward. He rode around the smoldering remains of the front of the establishment. The shop across the street was a mass of crackling flames; it would soon cave in too, then burn itself out.

He went to the church and rode slowly among those bodies, looking for signs of life, although the gaping, bloody holes in their heads promised little hope. He paused to look at a darkened cabin that stood surrounded by ponderosa pine and elm. Seeing no movement, he turned the Ovaro and rode to the saloon, where he dismounted and loose-reined the stallion to one of the hitching rails. Glancing back to the burning shop, he ambled to the saloon's swinging doors.

He held the doors open while pausing to gaze around the silent room. Only shards in the two lower corners of a rosewood frame testified that a grand mirror had moments ago adorned the wall behind the long bar. Not one piece of furniture stood upright, and all lamps save the one atop the piano were flameless.

The air still hung heavy with the pungent odor of gunpowder. From the lamp's soft glow, the big man counted six dead men among the toppled tables and chairs. Playing cards, poker chips, and money lay where they had fallen on the dark wood floor. Fargo lifted his gaze up the stairs.

With his Colt in one hand and the lamp in the other, he went upstairs and swung the first door open. A partially clad man lay sprawled on the floor. His outstretched right hand still groped for the holstered five-shot, single-action Joslyn army revolver on his gun belt draped over a chair. The man had a third eye, ugly red, of course, between the open and glazed brown two he'd been born with. Fargo backed out of the room.

The next door was also open. He stuck the lamp inside, swept his gaze over the unmade bed and onto the single straight-back chair. The absence of any clothing or a gun belt suggested the person may have gotten away. He went in and looked around anyway and found the room deserted.

He went down the hall to a closed door. Easing it open, he peered inside. In the lamp's light he saw the nude body of a shapely female lying bellydown, half on and half off a huge bed. Her chin all but touched the floor. Her long honey-colored hair splayed outward on the planks as though purposely arranged to add emphasis to her sensual pose. Fargo moved to the foot of the bed. Her long slim legs were apart, the right knee bent, tucked as though she were preparing to rise, and this accentuated her firm unblemished buttocks. He saw no blood.

He set the lamp on the small wash table next to the bed, then took her under the arms and lifted her to lie faceup on the bed. His gaze went down her length, noting the full breasts, soft convex belly with a deep dimple in its center, and bushy, curly pubic hair that matched that on her head.

Looking back to her prettily shaped face, he now saw the small lump at the hairline on her forehead, and the tip of her tongue barely showing between her wide lips.

He stepped to the porcelain washbowl and reached for a cloth to wet. His hearing, trail-trained and as acute as a wild creature, detected someone walking softly in the barroom below. He froze and listened.

Fargo drew his Colt, then eased out of the room and hugged the hallway wall leading to the upper landing. Peering around the corner, he saw the dim forms of two persons crossing to the stairs. The taller of the two carried a rifle. Before Fargo could warn them to stop and drop their weapons, they halted. There was a flash as the one with the rifle shot at him from the hip. Fargo ducked back in time and the slug chewed a hunk out of the corner of the wall.

A woman's voice cried, "You got him, Avis! You got him!"

"No, Avis, you missed," Fargo replied. "You're going to get killed wandering around in the dark with that rifle. Come on up and let's talk. There's an unconscious woman up here and you two might help me bring her around. Don't make me shoot you, ladies. Okay, Avis?"

Another slug slammed into the corner. A different

voice, obviously belonging to the one called Avis, quavered, "You stay away from my niece."

"Lady, I said she's hurt and needs help. Now, I'm not going to stand here all night and let you take potshots at me. The next time you shoot, I'm going to have to hurt both of you. So let me hear that rifle hit the floor, then come on up."

He listened to them whispering, then heard the thud when the rifle hit the boards.

The first voice said, "We only have the one rifle, mister, and it's on the floor. We're coming up to get my sister."

Fargo stepped from safety and watched the two women for signs of treachery as they came up to join him. Both wore high-collar dresses, the hems of which swept the floor. Both had badly beaten faces. The younger and shorter of the two had a swollen right eye, all but closed, and the taller, less shapely woman's thin lips were split. Fargo led them down the hall and into the room.

The younger woman's hands flew to her mouth to stifle a sharp gasp as she halted in the open doorway, but her companion rushed to the bed and drew the sheet up to the naked woman's neck. Glancing to Fargo, she censured, "Might have known you'd be the kind to violate an unconscious female." To the young woman she barked, "Catherine, don't just stand there gawking like an empty-headed schoolgirl. Fetch me a wet cloth." To her naked niece she asked softly, "Dora, it's me, honey, Aunt Avis. Me and Catherine are here to get you. Can you hear me, Dora?"

When Catherine handed Avis the wet cloth, Fargo spoke. "How did you ladies escape that gang of no-goods? Looks to me like you got caught and beat up. Who were those people, anyhow? They killed damn near everybody."

Avis shot him a hard glance. "Look, mister, leave the room or turn your back while we get Dora dressed." Without looking at her she told Catherine to find undergarments and a dress for Dora.

Fargo moved to a window opening onto the balcony and watched the reflections of the fire in what remained of the glass windows in the shop across the street. He heard Avis mutter, "Don't know what got into your mind to cause you to abandon the Lord for this sinful way of life in the first place. You've brought nothing but shame down on all of us. I can't wait to leave this horrible godforsaken place."

Fargo asked, "Why haven't you? I didn't see any fences."

"Dora here's my fence," she snapped. "We couldn't go and leave her behind. She's sinful, yes, but she can still be saved and lead a God-fearing, dutiful life. Pull those drawers up higher, Catherine, then help me work the dress down over her. Who are you, anyhow, mister, and what are you doing in this hellhole, besides visiting ladies' bedrooms?"

Fargo didn't answer right away. He thought about what the woman said. Avis was so attached to her bible teachings that she'd forgot how to enjoy life. The woman couldn't be more than thirty, and she sounded as though she hated men. He wondered if Catherine thought as Avis did. "Some call me the Trailsman and others Skye Fargo. I came to fetch two youngsters and take them to—"

Avis interrupted testily. "You can look now." When he turned to face her, she said, "You're big and strong. I'll say that for you, mister. You can carry Dora to our cabin, but I'll be watching where you put your hands."

Fargo cradled Dora in his muscular arms, making certain the grip met with Avis' approval, then followed

Catherine and marveled at the way her rolling ass swayed when she walked. He reckoned the sister in his arms weighed ten or fifteen pounds more than a hundred, and the darker-haired one in front of him about five pounds less. Fully clothed and standing in a downpour, he imagined their aunt might make it to an even hundred, but no more.

He looked at Avis' profile and thought she'd look half-decent—on the low side of pretty—were it not for the thin lips through which the woman spewed holy venom. He thought the somewhat-less-than-charming woman's chest could use a couple of pounds of mounded flesh in the right places. He glanced at her behind, which moved in quick twitches. He believed the cheeks, if released from their tight bindings, would be both pinched and hard, matching the set of her jaw.

Catherine sprinted ahead when they approached the cabin nestled among the ponderosas. She had two lamps burning when Fargo entered the spic-and-span abode. Avis hurried around him and opened a door. He stepped into a lady's bedroom dominated by a bright-yellow canopied four-poster with a pieced Log Cabin quilt and two soft-yellow pillows. After Avis pulled open the quilt, he bent and laid Dora on the white sheet.

Standing back, he suggested, "She'll be all right. On the way over, I felt her squirm a couple of times. Your niece will wake up with a bad headache and tell you what she saw and felt in hell." He grinned when Avis cut her slitted eyes to him sharply, then he left the room.

Coming into the living area, he noticed Catherine had unhooked the top three buttons on her dress and pulled the collar aside to reveal milk-white skin. Her brown eyes, he noted, were busy gazing at his arms and torso. Several times her curiosity drifted to his groin. Each time her eyes flared briefly.

He said, "How old are you? Sixteen?"

She glanced up at his eyes and blushed. "No. I'm four years younger than Dora. I'll be nineteen my next birthday. Aren't you afraid . . . traveling all alone out here?"

He sat at the kitchen table before answering. "No, I'm used to it. Fear gets a person dead out here. You sure you're coming up on nineteen? How come a man hasn't already claimed you for his wife?"

Catherine's blush deepened and she lowered her eyes, but Avis answered from where she stood in the bedroom doorway. "That's enough of that kind of talk, mister. I know what you're thinking. You're thinking you're a fox, and this is the henhouse, and you can do what you please. Well, mister, you got another think coming because this is the Lord's house. You're welcome in it as long as you behave right and proper. Catherine, button the front of that dress and go tend to your sister."

When the young woman hurried to obey, Avis came and sat across from Fargo.

"Kind of hard on her, aren't you, ma'am? She didn't say or do anything wrong or improper."

"Catherine's pure and innocent, mister. It's my duty to see she remains in that condition until—"

"How about yourself?" Fargo cut in.

Now Avis' cheeks pinkened as her dark eyes widened with surprise. She gulped and replied icily, "Sir, watch your language. How dare you question my, my, my, er—"

He saved her from tainting her tongue with the word "virginity" by butting in and remarking, "It's been my experience those who holler the loudest have the most to hide. Usually the exact opposite from their talk, but none of you have anything to worry about from me. I'm just passing through."

During the silence that ensued he watched the aunt

become increasingly fidgety. Avis clasped and unfolded her hands, rubbed her forearms, finally drew her bible before her, opened it, and began reading to herself.

Fargo pushed back from the table and moved to stand in the doorway to look in on Catherine and her sister.

Catherine said, "You said you came to fetch two youngsters. Which youngsters, mister? There aren't any children in Gully Town."

Fargo brought a folded piece of paper from a hip pocket. Catherine flinched and Avis sprung to her feet when he opened it and read, "Mr. Fargo. My wife and I hereby commission you to proceed to Gully Town near lower Sioux Indian territory to collect our two youngsters and bring them to us in San Francisco. Enclosed is $300 to defray any expenses. You are due another $300 upon safe delivery. Have them here by mid-August. The lady at the church is in charge of them." Glancing up, he added, "It's signed by Reverend James Hunnicutt. This is Gully Town, isn't it?"

Avis got to him a step before Catherine. She yanked the letter out of Fargo's fingers and both women read it again. Catherine gasped, "Auntie Avis, that's Pa's signature, all right. I'd know it anywhere."

"I can see," the aunt barked. "What I don't see is any reference to me going also. Apparently James doesn't care what happens to me. And after all I've done for . . ." The older woman handed back the letter and studied Fargo anew. Her shoulders sagged somewhat when she sighed and explained, "James and Daisy established the church here. When God told him to go to San Francisco and establish a church for those sinners, James told me to look after their daughters till they came back for them. Mister, that was six years ago. All this time we believed they were killed on the way to California. Not one word from them, mind you, not one, now this."

Fargo watched tears form in the corners of her eyes, then well, break, and trickle down her cheeks.

Catherine's hands folded at her bosom as her head tilted heavenward. She shouted, "Hallelujah, hallelujah, praise the Lord, I'm saved!" Tears of joy covered her cheeks when she hugged Fargo tightly and whispered, "When, oh, when, are we leaving?"

The big man answered, "Just as soon as I put an end to those five men. Settlers moving west have enough problems as is without falling easy prey to the likes of that bunch. What's worse, all they have to do is ride into an Indian settlement and kill a few Indians to put the Sioux on the warpath. Let that happen and those settlers, this town, and others like it will have real serious problems." Folding the letter and tucking it back in his hip pocket, he told them he was going back into town to check around.

Outside, he whistled for the Ovaro, mounted up, and rode to check for signs of life in the few other cabins he'd seen from the ridge. All but two of the homesites were deserted. In those two he found the people shot to death. "They're kill-crazy," he mumbled, walking back to the Ovaro. "Blood begets blood." He settled back into the saddle and headed for the saloon.

As he was coming onto the street, a shot rang out from the saloon. A geyser of dust sprouted up several feet to his left. He spurred the horse to a run. Fargo slid to the ground in front of the general store and rolled behind a water trough.

The rifleman's next bullet hammered into the far end of the trough. "Lousy shot," he muttered, and drew the Colt, then waited for the third shot to be fired. When it kicked up dust at least a yard from his head, he sprang to his feet. Sprinting toward the saloon, he fired four fast rounds toward the balcony area.

A scared voice shrilled, "Don't shoot me! I give up. Please don't kill me."

Fargo halted and raised the Colt to aim along the railing of the balcony. "Pitch that rifle down," he ordered, "then come and stand where I can see you."

A breech-loading Henry came up from out of the blackness at the back of the balcony and fell tumbling into the dirt. Fargo watched a short hatless man with large eyes step from the gloom, his hands raised. "Come on down," Fargo commanded. The man turned to leave through one of the two windows leading onto the balcony. Fargo stopped him, saying, "No, not that way. Come over the railing so I can see you."

The man quickly obeyed and crumpled into a ball when he dropped to the street. Fargo went to him before the man could recover. Yanking him to his feet by the shirt collar, Fargo snarled, "Damn fool, I could've killed you. Who are you and why were you shooting at me?" He let go of the collar and holstered his Colt.

"You ain't gonna kill me are you, mister?" the fellow asked in a nervous tone. "I don't know why I shot at you. Just scared, I guess, what with the killing and all." He glanced about the street and steadied his gaze on the few flames still licking up from the burning building. "Name's Jud Mott," he said. Turning, he nodded toward the saloon and added, "I work over there for Zack Hardisty, the owner of the saloon. Handyman work. Or I did till all this."

Fargo headed for the swinging doors and told Mott to follow him. Inside, he instructed Mott to light a lamp or two. Fargo went behind the bar and got two glasses and a bottle of red-eye from under the counter, then swept broken glass from the bar with his forearm and poured two drinks.

Jud righted a poker table and placed one of the burning lamps in the center of it, then set the other lamp on the piano next to the far wall.

Glancing among the dead bodies, Fargo said, "Come over and have a drink to calm those nerves. Your shaking makes me nervous, Mott."

The young man hurried to the bar, grabbed the glass, and emptied it in one gulp. The big man refilled it as he asked Mott to identify the dead. Jud pointed as he spoke. "That one, he's Al Ferguson, owner of the firearms place that got blowed to hell. We told him he shouldn't carry all that dynamite in stock. Over by the piano is Axel Gunderman. Axel, he has the livery and does vet and smithy work too. At least he did. Don't know what we're gonna do now that he's dead."

Jud Mott continued identifying the corpses and reciting what they did for a living. Fargo learned Davey Bloxom was from the Rocking-3 ranch to the south, a long ride's distance, and Benjamin "Bennie" Tatum came from the Lazy Two 6 in the same direction, only farther south. Both were in town to play a little poker and drink a few whiskeys and visit Satisfied. The fat man lying in a heap in the pool of blood behind the bar was Rory Peters, Zack's bartender.

"All good men," Mott sighed at the end. "Just before them bastards rode in and started shooting up the place, killing everyone and all, Ferguson was showing something all secretlike to Axel. Whatever it was he was holding made old Axel's eyes get big. Both of 'em, they was excited."

"There's a dead man in the room upstairs, first door to the right," Fargo said.

"That'd be Zack," Mott replied, and looked up the stairs. "What am I gonna do for a job now?"

Fargo poured each a fresh drink before asking about

the plunderers. Mott gulped and said, "Why, mister, they're the Bible Boys. Mean sons of bitches, they are."

The big man watched him guzzle from the glass and remarked, "Never heard of them. How long have they been burning and killing and terrorizing folks in these parts?"

"You ain't never heard of the Bible Boys?" Mott gasped. His big eyes showed his surprise. When Fargo's head shook, Mott continued. "They're from somewhere in Arkansas, or so we understand. Ten of 'em in all, counting the young uns too little to hold a gun, and their ma, Hagar Hanks. That's their name, you know, Hanks. I only know some of their first names. Noah, he's the father. Then there's Matthew and Luke. They all got names right out of the bible. That's why they're called the Bible Boys. How many of 'em rode into Gully Town? I only saw three. The two who rode in the saloon here, then I saw one other later. But from all the shooting I knew there had to be more."

"Five in all," Fargo answered. "How did you manage to escape?"

"Out the back," Mott replied.

Fargo sipped and listened to Jud relate how he ran and dived into a huge bed of tall sagebrush well behind the saloon. Once he was sure none of the Bible Boys were coming after him to gun him down in cold blood, he got up and ran far into the night.

"After they left, I moseyed on back and took Bennie's rifle with me when I went to the balcony to look around. That's when I saw you and thought they was coming back. I ain't a very good shot, am I, mister?"

"Very poor, in fact," Fargo replied through an easy grin. "But you'll make a better saloon keeper. I'm giving the place to you. You can give me free room and board

26

and all the whiskey I can hold anytime I'm passing through."

"You mean that, mister? This here saloon is mine? Mine to keep and fix up like I please? Yessiree Bob, you can have any room you want, anytime."

Fargo watched him look about his new ownership as though seeing the saloon for the first time. "There's one more condition, kid. Dora. She doesn't work here any longer. Now toss down another drink and go out and start hauling in the dead bodies. Find a wagon. Have to bury the dead or else they'll rot and the stench will drive us out of town. I'll drag these in the saloon out into the street and you can help me load them in the wagon."

While Jud hurried out to comply, Fargo went upstairs, carried Zack Hardisty outside, and dumped him in the street, then he came back inside and dragged the others out. The last to go was the arms dealer, Al Ferguson. While dragging him by the ankles, Fargo noticed a small stone fall from the dead man's pocket and tumble under a chair. He released his grip, stooped, picked up the object, and took it to the lamp on the piano. Inspecting the small stone, he recognized it as a gold nugget.

Fargo cocked his head and a puzzled frown appeared on his chiseled face, for he knew of no gold in these parts.

2

A blazing sun peeked over the eastern horizon. Its first rays illuminated Avis in a golden aura that somehow escaped adorning Catherine, who stood next to her at the end of the common grave Fargo and Mott had dug. Tears of anguish marred the younger woman's pretty face.

Avis watched the two men remove the dead, one at a time, from the seed wagon. Mott had borrowed the Owensboro from Gunderman's place just east of town. With little respect they dropped the blood-splattered bodies into the waiting pit. "Careful, Mr. Fargo," Avis reminded haughtily. "Show some respect for our dear departed. Remember, God is watching."

The two dog-tired men ignored her reproach and continued as before. One of the women from the two wagons by the church was lowered last. The two sweat-drenched men stood back to rest and watched Avis send the dear departed on their way. She stiffened, straightened her shoulders, opened her bible to the twenty-third psalm, and began reading. "The Lord is my shepherd . . ."

Mott shifted his weight from one foot to the other throughout her fifteen-minute sermon, which included passages about mansions in the sky, dust to dust, He maketh me lie down, something about thy staff, and man is born out of sin. There was more, but Fargo believed Mott didn't hear it because of the many flies buzzing around their sweaty heads. Fargo searched the western horizon for signs of impending rain.

When Avis announced, "Amen," Mott immediately picked up his shovel and went to work. He had other important business to attend to at his new saloon.

Shoveling on the last spade of soil, Fargo inquired about Dora. "She's awake, Mr. Fargo," Avis replied, "but she isn't well. Will you take me with her and Catherine?"

"If you wish. What do you mean she isn't well?"

Avis glowered at him, spoke coldly. "Sir, Reverend Hunnicutt has paid you a handsome fee to take us to California. I think you should honor his commission and earn your pay. You are to abandon your idiotic idea about going after those horrible people and leave with us immediately." Walking away, she ordered Catherine, "Come along, child. We must pack our few belongings for the journey," as though Fargo had no say in the matter.

When Catherine looked at him questioningly, he told Avis, "You can pack if you want, but none of it will leave Gully Town. While I'm away, all three of you better find a couple of changes of riding britches because you'll damn sure need and want them where we're going."

Avis turned and placed her hands on her hips when he spoke to Mott. "Round up bedrolls for them. Also, see to it they have something to eat and drink from. While you're at it, make damn sure there's plenty of coffee."

Shifting his eyes to Avis, Fargo promised, "From now on you three take orders from me, not give them."

"Oh?" she began. "And what if—"

"No 'if' to it, ma'am," Fargo interrupted dryly. "You'll do as I say, or I'll leave you behind. Give me any mouth problems on the way, I'll leave you for the Indians. Your choice, ma'am. Those are my trail rules." He turned to Jud Mott and nodded toward the saloon.

As they walked away, Avis' hard voice shouted, "Not only are you stupid, Mr. Fargo, you're insensitive."

He ignored her bitterness for the moment and said to Mott, "I want you to saddle up and ride out to those two ranches to let the hands know what happened here last night. Tell them we've already buried their dead. Mention that I'm going to find their killers and put an end to their marauding activities. While you're at it, say I said they should be especially alert for Indians till I come back and say everything's okay."

"Er, er, what if you don't come back, sir?"

Fargo just looked at him amusedly, shook his head, turned back, and headed for the women's cabin. Mott gulped and hurried to the livery.

The big man didn't bother to knock before entering. They might as well start getting used to his surprise appearances here and now in broad daylight rather than later in the middle of the night on the trail. Then there would be no privacy.

He closed the door, then stood with his back to it while he watched and listened to the three women, none of whom noticed his entrance. All three women stood facing one another. Avis and Catherine were speaking at the same time, quoting stretches of Scripture from their bibles which first one then the other used as an accusative finger when pointing at Dora for added emphasis.

Dora wore a sheer nightgown that hid nothing. She had her hands on her hips, her shoulders thrown back. The defiant stance only thrust her rounded breasts out and up toward her venomous aunt's drawn face. Her shapely buttocks were high and pronounced. Fargo wondered what the trio would look like dressed in Levi's and shirts.

Catherine saw him first and instantly fell silent. She stared at him as though she'd been caught doing something wrong. Dora noticed her stare and followed it, but Avis finished her current admonishment before slamming her bible shut and doing likewise. Fargo did not miss the sudden delight that flashed in Dora's eyes when she looked at him, or the blush that spread across her sister's cheeks, or the icy stare leveled on him by their aunt.

Dora broke the silence, saying, "You must be Skye Fargo. Catherine said you found me and brought me here. Thanks."

He walked to join them and kept his gaze fixed on Dora's dark areolae beneath the twin peaks on her gown. He knew she didn't mind, and he didn't care if the other two did. "You don't look sick," he offered, and glanced at Avis.

"I owe you, Fargo," Dora said, "and I always pay my debts. I can and will pay you here and now, or later. Maybe both."

"Dora," Avis cried, her eyes bristling with hellfire. "Shame on you, child, for suggesting such a thing."

Fargo's lake-blue eyes moved from the aunt's firm-set jaw to Catherine's swollen eye, then settled on Dora's lips. "Ma'am, you don't owe me anything," he replied, and looked into her eyes. He saw her gaze sweeping over his upper torso, shoulders, and arms. "But I would take it kindly if one of you ladies will make me a breakfast." Cutting his eyes to Avis, he advised, "I'll be riding out at dawn and won't have time to stop to cook. You might fry me a cut-up chicken to eat on the way."

Avis spat, "No! We'll be glad to feed you on the trail, Mr. Fargo. We'll have our things in the buckboard within the hour. There isn't time to cook."

"Have it your way, ma'am," he answered. He turned for the front door.

"No! Wait," Dora said, incensed. "I'll fix you a breakfast, Fargo. Catherine, you go get a chicken."

He turned back and went to the table. Avis grabbed Catherine by her arm and pulled her into their bedroom. The aunt slammed the door, saying, "Don't listen to her."

Dora asked, "How many eggs, big man?"

"Three. Scrambled hard, please."

She smiled. "Hard, huh? Like everything else I'm seeing on you. I guess I'm not the first woman to tell you you're handsome and powerful. Can't wait to pay you, big man." She drew her gaze off his chiseled face and stepped to the stove.

Fargo watched her inverted heart-shaped ass jiggle while she busied herself at the stove. He said, "So you'll know, I told that kid, Jud Mott, the saloon's now his. I also told him not to let you come back in the place."

Dora glanced over her left shoulder at him and pursed her lips. "Oh?" she finally mused. "Why's that, Fargo? Are you saying I'm your private property from now on?"

"Hardly. I just don't want to have to come looking for you when I get back. And, who knows, I may come back in the middle of the night. Don't burn those eggs, ma'am."

Dora set a platter of scrambled eggs with crisp fried bacon in front of him, then a pan of warmed-over biscuits, butter, and molasses next to the cup of steaming coffee. Sitting across from him, she rested her elbows on the table and her chin in her hands. "What I do is my business, Skye Fargo. If I want to go back to the saloon, I will. And I might do just that."

He ate from the platter and drank from the cup first, then answered, "Certainly, ma'am. Just remember this. You'll be in this cabin when I return or we leave without you. I'll tell the reverend you were too busy being a whore to come to California."

"You wouldn't."

Fargo didn't answer. He pushed back from the table, stood, downed the last of the black coffee from his cup, then moved for the door.

Dora rose and ran to stop him. Wedging herself between him and the door, she looked up into his eyes and whispered, "I'll be here waiting for you." Rising onto the tips of her toes, she squeezed his muscular arms, pressed her parted lips to his, and moaned, "God, yes, I'll be waiting."

Fargo met her probing tongue with his own as he cupped her heaving breasts in his hands and applied firm pressure. When she lowered a hand to his groin, he broke the passionate kiss and held her back from him. "No, not now," he said softly.

"When?" she asked, and he saw a pleading in her eyes.

"Later. Right now I have other things to tend to."

Dora's shoulders sagged in disappointment. She stepped aside to let him pass. He patted her ass as he went through the doorway. "Later."

Fargo rode to the livery, where he unsaddled the big Ovaro and removed the bridle. While the horse fed on oats, Fargo curried it, cleaned its hooves, and picked around the frogs, then tightened its right fore shoe. After checking to make sure his mount had plenty of oats in the feed bucket, he left for the saloon.

Upon entering, he went behind the bar, got a fresh bottle of whiskey and a glass, and took both with him upstairs. He looked inside all the rooms before he went inside Dora's and walked to the windows overlooking the balcony and street. Parting the flimsy curtains, he glanced about, then looked up the sheer rocky wall. His gaze settled on the rim of the ridge where he'd stood the previous evening. So close, but so far, he thought.

He turned away, released the curtain, and stepped to the dresser. Opening a drawer, he fingered her soft clean undergarments, brought a frilly pair of drawers to his face, and sniffed the perfume and powder that emanated from the thin black material. He replaced them, shut the drawer, and stepped to her bed.

As he removed his outer garments, boots, and hat, he listened to the silence and wondered how far he'd have to chase the Bible Boys before finding and killing them. He continued the thought as he poured a drink, then reclined on the bed to sip from it. Dora's sweet scent on the bed caressed his head and face, washed away his thoughts of violence, and replaced them with thoughts of her supple body.

Fargo drifted into sleep seeing her naked, lying unconscious, half on, half off the bed.

His wild-creature hearing snapped his eyes open. His right hand involuntarily reached for the Colt under his pillow as he sat up. He glanced first to the windows, then to the closed door. Easing off the bed, he heard movement down in the saloon, then Mott's high-pitched voice say, "Gotta get my saloon fixed up for business." The kid continued talking aloud to himself as he went about righting tables and chairs.

Fargo holstered the Colt and got dressed. Downstairs, he poured a fresh drink and asked Jud how they took it at the ranches.

"Well, sir, I guess you could say they're hopping mad. They said you can count on 'em to ride with you if you want their help. But the men in the bunkhouses, they didn't take it kindly when I told 'em what you said 'bout not letting Satisfied work no more."

Fargo stood with his back resting against the edge of

the bar while he watched Mott hurry to get the room in order before the sun lowered completely. "That's twice now I've heard you call her Satisfied. You want to explain that to me?"

Mott chuckled. "I wasn't around at the time, but I've heard the story told enough times to believe it. She'd been getting flat on her back for only a couple of months when some ranchhands brung this kid to the saloon for a night of fun. One of the guys got Dora aside and told her the kid never done it before. He asked her to show him how. She took him up to her room and closed the door, but two of the men peeked through the keyhole to watch 'em.

"They say that kid was red as a beet all over, what with blushing and all when she took off his clothes. Anyhow, she did everything to that boy. Those two watching snickered their heads off when he took to grunting, groaning, claiming she was tearing it plumb off, that it hurt like blazes. She just kept bouncing him up and down with her legs locked around his waist so's he couldn't get away. Said he screamed, 'Sumpin's burning inside me, lady! I feel funny inside down there! You're killing me, lady!'

"Said his back arched way up, shut his eyes real tight, and screamed real loud at the end. Then he went limp as a dishrag and couldn't move for an hour. Just laid there with a big smile on his face while he looked at her all dreamy-eyed. Said she patted his new tool and asked if he got satisfied.

"After that, everbody started calling her Satisfied. Get it, mister? Satisfied? Dora, she can make any man feel satisfied."

When Fargo asked what happened to the kid after that, Mott told him he couldn't get enough of being satisfied. "Ten wagons filled with settlers stopped at Gully

Town one day just before dark. Must've been twenty or more young females—you know, sixteen or so—ripe and ready to pluck. The kid nearly went out of his mind tending to their needs. One of 'em's pa caught 'em doing it in the church. He blowed the kid's head off. I say one thing, though: that boy went to heaven or hell feeling mighty satisfied." Mott grinned and changed the subject. Pointing to a basket on the far end of the bar, he said, "The Lazy Two Six butchered a beef. They sent us a few steaks. There's a place to cook 'em out back. I'll be glad to throw a couple on the fire soon as I finish in here."

"You stay with your cleaning up. I'll start things." Fargo fetched the basket of meat and went out back, where he found the fire pit and iron grate. After cleaning both, he made a fire, then sat to wait for the wood to turn to embers.

Mott came out and joined him just as he was laying two large, thick T-bone steaks on the grill. While the steaks sizzled, Fargo questioned Jud about something the young man mentioned the night before. "I'm curious, Mott. When was the last time any Indians came to Gully Town?"

Jud answered without forethought, "Yesterday afternoon. Four Sioux braves rode in on ponies to buy whiskey. Zack, he let 'em have eight bottles."

"Eight? Damn, kid, where you reckon they got that much money? Have the Sioux been attacking wagon trains in this area lately?"

"No, sir, they ain't. It's been quiet 'round these parts for a long time. They don't mess with us, and we leave 'em alone. But they had money, though. They paid Al Ferguson's place a visit before coming over to the saloon for whiskey. Al, he got some of their money too. They was all carrying brand-new Spencer fifty-twos. Al had several in stock."

"Oh? What band were they from? Which way did they go when they left?"

"Oglala Sioux. They rode north, toward forbidden territory, at least it is to us whites. The Black Hills."

Fargo's right hand dipped into his pant's pocket and his fingers toyed with the gold nugget that had escaped from Ferguson's pocket.

He thought about that while he carved off bites of the T-bone. The Indians had probably traded the nugget to Ferguson for rifles and enough cash to buy the whiskey. The nugget would be the secret something that Mott saw Ferguson show Gunderman.

Fargo turned his head to face north. He wondered where the Sioux got the nugget.

3

Beyond the two windows in the upstairs room a bright half-moon looked down from where it hung three-quarters high above the southeastern horizon in a cloudless hot sky. The moonbeams bathed the balcony and all of Gully Town in gray-white serenity. A playful zephyr skipped onto the balcony, kissed the sheer curtains, and billowed them before swirling on its way. On the bullet-nicked boulder atop the ridge sat a coyote.

Fargo lay sprawled facedown, asleep on the love-scented huge bed. His muscled narrow buttock cheeks, powerful wide back and shoulders, strong arms, thighs, and legs glistened from the light film of perspiration that covered his body. His slow, even breaths made no sound. Were it not for the barely noticeable, equally slow, even rise and fall of his back at the lower rib cage he would have appeared dead.

The coyote angled its eyes at the moon and howled mournfully. Fargo's eyes snapped open instantly. His right hand snaked under the pillow and grasped the handle of the Colt. He looked through the still curtains, then relaxed when the coyote howled again. He turned his head to face the door and go back to sleep. Through partially closed eyes, he saw someone standing next to the open door. Fully awake now, and keenly alert, he tightened his grip on the Colt and laid a fingertip on its trigger.

He was easing the gun out from under the pillow when the silhouette spoke. "Don't shoot, big man. It's me, Satisfied." As he propped up on an elbow, she stepped from the wall and came to look down on him. "I've come to pay my debt, and I won't take no for an answer."

Fargo watched her hands raise to her shoulders, pull open the collar of her nightdress, then wiggle the sheer white garment down her body and onto the wood floor. She stood naked before him, her eyes savoring his muscular body. Her hands cupped her breasts, squeezed on them, the forefingers and thumbs teased the large areolae and pink nipples until the latter perked hard and erect. "Roll over, big man. Let me see what I have imagined and what I shall pay."

As he turned onto his back, his hand released the Colt, but his gaze stayed fixed on her eyes, which grew quite wide and filled with delight as they roamed down his muscular torso to settle on his mighty yet unawake member.

"Jesus, Fargo, what have I lucked into this time?" she purred. She knelt at his waist on the bed. Her breath quickened as her right palm slid caressively over his muscled chest and shoulders. Her left found and curled partially around his swelling girth. Keeping the grip, she bent parted, wettened lips to his mouth and kissed him hungrily, as though this was the first and last time for her, as though she wanted to remember the thrill forever.

His tongue darted past hers and captured it in a swirling motion and sucked its sweetness. She moaned lowly, parted her lips full open, and took his mouth in hers. Her body trembled with anticipation. She gasped uncontrollably, the quick hot breaths filling Fargo's mouth.

The hand on his great member pumped, squeezed, and stroked again. His hands meshed into her long honey-colored hair, and he pulled her head back. Dora pressed her left nipple between his hot wet lips, moved it across several times, and moaned, "Suck, Fargo. Oh, God, yes, big man, suck them off, please."

He swirled his tongue around the firm nipple, circled the brownish-pink areolae a few times, then took in as much of the quivering breast as his mouth could hold and sucked the firm mound while she gasped continuously, "Where, oh, where have you been? Oh, my God, that's good . . . so good . . . take its twin, big man . . . take it too. Suck them off, Fargo, please, please, suck them off . . . aaeeiiii!"

Fargo's left hand drew her left breast against the right, brought the two nipples as close as possible, then took them both between his lips and nibbled on them, first the left, then the right. The excited young woman shrieked her ecstasy, "I'm in heaven, I'm in beautiful heaven . . . oh, God, this is wonderful."

When he came off the swollen breasts to take a fresh breath, Dora's salivating mouth kissed down his muscled torso, her hot tongue pausing at his navel to swish around inside it, then lowering quickly to curl along the throbbing hot length of his manliness. He felt her left hand grip his scrotum and begin a gentle massage as the other held his length at its base. She guided the swollen summit to her mouth. Then her wet lips slipped over and down it slowly and paused to tighten at the base of his crown, which filled her mouth. He felt her hot tongue circling, darting through and parting the thin slit at the crest, massaging the entire head of it.

She gurgled unceasingly as her hot lips moved up and down, forcing him deeper and deeper inside her ample aperture, unable to drive past her fingers wrapped tightly around his superb diameter as far as they could reach. He lifted her by the waist, bent her knees to straddle his chest, and coaxed her honey-colored bush to his lips. When his probing tongue parted her swollen entrance, he felt her lips leave his member. Dora screamed, "Take me, Fargo! Oh, Jesus, take me now!"

But he wasn't yet ready to let this wildcat go. He held her firmly by the hips and pressed her forcefully downward. She screamed again, began gyrating her hips, mashing her begging lower opening across and up and down his eager lips, shuddering with each deep probe he made, gasping when he withdrew.

Breathing heavily, Dora swung around to face him and maintained her straddling position. She placed his hands over her breasts and set him to squeezing and pulling on them, then raised high on her knees. Using both hands, she guided the enormous, radiant crimson prow into her eager love nook.

As it entered, her eyes became wide and her mouth gaped, her lips trembling with pleasurable disbelief. Her head tilted way back and her back arched as her joy exploded. "Yes, oh, Jesus, yes!" He heard her gulp twice before feeling her Venus' glove contract down and swallow his enormous length. Dora fell toward him groaning rapturously, whimpering, "Split me, big man, split me wide open. Oh, God, Fargo, you're in places where no man has been. I want it all . . . all of it."

He took her by the hips and lunged upward as he forced her wet V down to bottom out at the stout base of his length. She screamed, "Aaeeiiii! Aaeeiiii," and rejoiced, "So big . . . so long . . . so damn heavy! Yes, yes, oh, Jesus, yes, that's it."

She grunted with pleasure, and her hips rose and fell beneath his strong grip. With each downward movement he felt her buttocks tense as she tried to force him one more inch deeper inside the lubricious opening. His member stiffened extra hard in prelude to erupting. She reached behind her and massaged the tightened bag again, mewing, "Wait for me, Fargo. Please not now, big man. Wait for me . . . I'm nearly th—"

He fused her crotch to his as the hot gusher burst from deep within him and flooded her depths. She gasped loudly when the burning flow triggered her own fulfilling orgasm, then yelped with added bliss when her many contractions began squeezing, milking out the final hot drops.

When it was over and he limbered, she fell forward, curled her arms around his powerful neck, and kissed his muscular chest, shoulders, and throat. Panting, she whispered, "Satisfied?"

He chuckled. "For the moment, yes."

She bit him on the chin. "You mean you aren't through? C'mon, Fargo, admit mine was the wildest ride you ever had. Surely you can't get it—"

He slapped her ass and cut her off, saying, "There was this she-grizzly that got in my bedroll one night and—"

She bit him again, this time on a cheek. "Don't joke with me, Fargo. I know any man built like you—and I do mean built in all the right places—has all the women he wants. So, you can make comparisons. How do I fit in with the best you've wrestled with?"

"Well, let's see," he began. "There was a young woman in Colorado high country who—"

"I don't want to hear about her," Dora snapped. "If I'm not number one on your long list, then—"

He put a finger to her lips. "I was going to say she tried real hard to satisfy me but faded dismally at the end. Satisfied?"

"Yeah. I guess so. You aren't going to tell me, are you?"

"Nope. I don't discuss other females with the one lying in bed with me."

"Well, I do. And this is as good a time as any to warn you about my sister and Aunt Avis, seeing how's it looks like I'm going to have to share you with them on the way to California."

"What do you mean by share?" Fargo asked, surprise laced in the tone.

"All I'm saying is, don't get caught alone with either one of them. Don't let those bibles they carry around fool you for one minute. Avis, especially Avis, would gladly give her eye teeth to have you crush her nakedness beneath all your muscles."

"So, why should I be bothered by her? Seems like I can handle—"

Dora hastened to interrupt. Shaking her head, she said, "You men simply do not understand us women. Lying in bed with men is all we think about. Avis is no different. I can promise that if you winked at her, she'd start peeling off her clothes."

"I'll make it a point to be careful that I don't wink when she's around. Now, what about your sister?"

"Catherine is one fling in the hay away from being a virgin. Thanks to a good-looking young man on a wagon heading west. She spread her legs for him when she was fifteen in hopes he'd take her with him. All he did was laugh at her. Since then, she attached herself to Avis and took her attitude. But I know my sister. She's got an itch between her big toes that needs scratching real bad. Had that same bad itch myself. Only I got mine scratched over in the saloon. So, Fargo, you best be wary of darling Catherine on dark nights. Both of them, for that matter."

"I will. And yourself?"

"Big man, you can count on me coming at you every

chance I get, especially after what we just did. Dammit, Fargo, I can't leave a body like yours alone. Not when I have to look at it day and night. That saddle's going to keep my legs spread apart. If that isn't sexy enough, the constant rubbing on it's going to make my juices flow."

"Look, Dora, don't get me wrong. I'm not out to save any woman for another man, but I do think you should ease off on the passion and start thinking about marriage. At the rate you're hopping in bed, you'll be worn out in a few years, then no man will want you. Nobody in San Francisco knows what you've been doing. Keep your past hidden in a closet. Good-looking woman like you will find it easy to marry the right man and live happily ever after."

She sat up and stared at him, disbelief flashing in her eyes. "Are you saying we aren't going to—?"

He answered by pushing her onto her back and rolling on top of her. The coyote, Avis, and Catherine listened to a new and different howling. All three found sleep impossible.

Dawn was near when the Trailsman awakened. He slipped out of bed without disturbing Dora's sound sleep, collected his clothes, gun belt, and the Sharps, all of which he took downstairs. He dressed on the porch below the balcony. Sitting to pull on his boots, he listened to the early-morning sounds: a rooster crowed, a horse whinnied. When they quietened, he heard the soft gurgles of the stream passing over a shallow, rocky bottom. He glanced to the bright morning star, then stood and walked to the livery to make the pinto ready for travel. Fifteen minutes later, Fargo rode south, out of Gully Town.

Though he knew it would be a futile exercise, he still watched for signs of the Bible Boys even though they had left in the opposite direction. All he saw were three-day-old tracks left by the wagons parked at the church.

At ten o'clock he came to the junction where the trail to Gully Town met the east-west artery settlers followed moving west. He turned west with his back to the warm July morning sun and tracked alongside the ruts and hoofprints he saw occasionally in the barren places among the tall prairie grass. Fargo's experienced eyes noted it had been a while since the last wagons passed this way.

The blazing white sun was directly overhead when he reined the Ovaro to a halt to study a clear stretch of soil in front of him. In addition to the tracks left by the wagon teams he'd been following, he counted five other sets of hoofprints. All five were shod, all fresher than the others, and riding west. Encouraged, he spurred the pinto into a lope and kept close watch on the ground signs left by the riders.

Two hours later he saw the remains of a small campfire beside the trail. Fargo dismounted to have a closer look. The condition of the coals, ashes, and charred ends of firewood told Fargo the fire had burned itself out less than twenty-four hours ago. They stopped here to catch a few winks of sleep, he mused to himself. Moving back to the Ovaro, he looked west through the shimmering heat waves. The grizzled Irishman's trading post was that way, just over the horizon, about eighteen hours' riding time. He slipped up onto the saddle and nudged the pinto to canter.

Twice he paused in the blistering heat to dismount and let the horse rest and cool down, then he pressed on at the same steady gait. At sundown he stopped to eat and catch a few winks. He plucked two handfuls of dark blue berries from a stand of chokecherry bushes nearby, then stretched out on his bedroll to eat them while staring up at the stars. He reckoned he could arrive at the trading post early the next morning if he was back in the saddle by midnight. The big man closed his eyes and willed himself to sleep.

An inner clock awakened him to see the Big Dipper had lowered from its previous location in the heavens. The new position clearly indicated the hour was nearing midnight. Again he ate from the chokecherry bushes, then mounted up and rode toward the lower star on the handle of the Big Dipper.

He topped a slight rise and halted on the knoll of buffalo grass. Although the dawn's first light was faint and the western horizon quite dim, he nonetheless saw the thin, wispy column of smoke rising in the distance. He urged the Ovaro toward the column of smoke less than an hour's ride away.

Off to his left stood a large herd of the Indian's sacred bulls. The buffalo ignored him as they grazed. To his right loomed the dark foothills of the Siouan's holiest of all holy lands, He Sapa, the sacred Black Hills, the one region within Sioux territory where the white man was forbidden to set foot.

He glanced in that direction and recalled the time he'd sat in a circle with Brules. He'd stared into the fire at its center while one of them warned him He Sapa was *wakan*. While he knew enough of the Sioux language and their hand signs to communicate with them, he'd never heard the word *"wakan."* It took some intense listening and watching on his part, but he eventually understood the warrior meant the hills were supernatural.

Skye Fargo could appreciate their concern not to violate their demands and enter the region. They feared the white man would desecrate their Garden of Eden, as he had desecrated all other places he trod. Fargo had told his Brule friends not to worry, that he would respect their wishes and warnings and not go into He Sapa, that there were plenty of other places he'd not yet seen or visited. They smiled their pleasure.

Then one of the Brule warriors had filled a long-stem pipe from which they all smoked to seal what they had done and said and to send those acts and words in the wisps of smoke up into the universe to Wakan Tanka, God.

Now he halted on a low rise to consider not one but two other kinds of wispy smoke, neither of which was sending messages to God. One, the most pronounced, came from the trading post's chimney. The lesser rose from the cluster of pine and oak a short walk from the trading post, which included Elmer Dugan and Little Feather's living quarters.

Shifting his studious gaze to the corral this side of the stand of trees and well behind Dugan's place, he counted seven horses, an Indian pony, and four mules. That was five horses more than Elmer Dugan was ever known to keep. He noticed one of them was the same big dun he'd seen ridden into the saloon.

Fargo wondered if Elmer and his woman, Little Feather, were still alive. He concluded they were. Both were too damn mean and tough to be taken by this lot. Little Feather alone could take out five men in short order and not even work up a sweat while doing it. And Fargo had seen Dugan put seven big sons of bitches on the floor. Still, the bastards might have caught them by surprise.

He backed the Ovaro off the rise and began a wide circle to put him on the far side of the trees and trading post. Once he reached that point, he angled the pinto straight for the gray-white smoke rising from within the trees. He knew the campfire would probably be on one of the banks of the creek that coursed down out of the foothills, meandered through the trees, passed west of the post, then vanished into the grasslands.

Fargo approached at a walk with his hand resting on the

handle of the Colt, ready to grasp and fire it on a split second's notice if they spotted him. But luck was with him this morning. He rode unnoticed into a deep gulch. Only his head showed above the sides of the ravine. He was close, damn close, and clearly saw three of the Bible Boys yawning and stretching awake. A fourth stood at the creek with the front of his long johns open. The tall lanky man scratched his butt while relieving himself into the creek. Fargo was also close enough to hear bits of their conversation. The one fouling the water remarked in a tinny voice, "I got six back in Gully. How many'd you get, Luke? One?" He laughed when he said it.

Fargo presumed it was Luke's whiny voice that answered, "Two more'n you did. Ain't that right, Pa? I did get eight, didn't I?"

Pa's raspy voice answered, "Hell, I don't keep count, boy. But it was a bunch, when you add in the women. Only found one in the saloon, but she took off up the stairs before I could shoot her. Jez went after her. Matt, why don't you stop draining your lizard and start the bacon frying? It's gonna take us better part of eight hours to get to Hubbard's Crossing."

Fargo glanced about to spot the fifth man and saw no evidence of him. Fargo reckoned the late-sleeper was snoozing somewhere among the cluster of young cedars between two tall pines on the far side of the creek. Not that it mattered for him to see all five; they were as good as dead.

Matt chuckled as he spoke to the others behind him. "Hubbard's ain't going nowhere. Seeing's how we be so close, why don't we go find us one of them Indian villages and kill a few of 'em, maybe get some purdies to take back to Ma and the young uns. Hell, Pa, they never get to have no fun like us."

Luke's voice said, "Good idea, Matt. While we're at it, we could get us a few of them young Injun gals, see if they do it same as white girls. Anything wrong with that, Pa? We can always kill 'em after. Huh, Pa?''

Fargo had seen and heard all he wanted. He patted the Ovaro's strong neck, withdrew the Sharps from its saddle case, checked to make sure a round was chambered; then, holding it like a handgun in his left hand, he drew the Colt with his right and dug his heels into the pinto's flanks. The big horse exploded out of the gulch.

The Trailsman rode in squeezing both triggers. The Sharps' bullet tore a nasty hole in Matt's forehead before he could take his hands from his butt. The impact lifted him off the ground, hurled him backward.

The other three came off their bedrolls with weapons in hand, running crouched to find cover in the thicket of trees.

Fargo dropped one with the Colt. The young man slammed into the trunk of a pine, grabbed it momentarily, then sunk to his knees and toppled backward.

The other two made it to safety and laid down blistering return fire with their rifles and revolvers.

Fargo veered the Ovaro to the right and raced for the trading post. As he did, he saw the fifth gang member, the short one who rode the big dun, run from the blind side of the trading post, race through the corral, and dive head-long into the tall grass behind it.

That Bible Boy fired two rifle shots at Fargo before he came alongside the log cabin, slid from the saddle, and took cover between it and a long, low boulder next to it. Bullets chewed into the cabin or kissed off the boulder near his head as he calmly reloaded his weapons and assessed the situation.

He turned his head to face the cabin and shouted, "Hey, in there! It's me, Fargo! Get your lazy ass out here, Elmer, and give me a hand."

There was no reply from inside.

Four slugs ricocheted off the boulder and thudded into the logs. All came from the same general direction, the trees. Fargo concluded—and rightly so—that he was out of the fifth renegade's field of fire, not that it mattered, because the other two had successfully pinned him down. To leave the stone was tantamount to committing suicide, to stay only prolonged the danger. Whether or not they realized it, they truly did have him between a rock and a hard place, and the big man didn't like it one damn bit.

The position, while relatively safe, forced him to watch in three directions. He had to keep an eye on both corners of the trading post in order to spot the man in the grass if he should be so bold as to dare a surprise confrontation. Fargo hoped that would be the case. He also had to consider those hiding in the trees beyond the boulder. Actually, he hoped all three would come in firing. Once they exposed themselves, all would go down, each weighing one bullet heavier.

There was only one sure way for him to force them out into the open. Stay down and the power of curiosity would eventually make one or more come to see if he was dead. Fargo waited.

At high noon not another shot had been fired after the four that skimmed across the top of the boulder. Fargo stared up at the brilliant diffused white orb baking him and silently begged for a torrential downpour to somehow manifest itself. Not only was it ungodly hot, but not a breath of air stirred.

Pa Hanks shouted, "Warm enough fer you behind that rock, mister? It's real shady over here."

"Yeah," a new voice hollered, "and we got plenty of cool water too. Want us to bring you a pail of it, mister?"

He listened to them laugh while he refused to drag his tongue across his parched lips to wet them. They were taunting him, hoping he would give up and stand so they could kill him. He turned his face away from the sun, said nothing.

Much later the blazing sun in decline lowered to the point where a shadow appeared on his side of the huge stone. Fargo alternated watching both corners of the trading post and the shadow creeping toward him. When the shadow lengthened enough to make it possible, he put his mouth and nose in it and inhaled deeply of the noticeably cooler air.

Pa Hanks shouted again, "Hey, over thar behind the horses! Move this way a mite and see if you can spot him and tell if he's daid or not."

Fargo listened for a reply but heard none. Neither did he believe Old Man Hanks meant what he said. This too was a sham cleverly designed to worry him to the point where he'd commit an error in judgment. Noah Hanks was probably motioning his boy to stay at the corral. You don't toy with success in a safe standoff. Fargo kept his face in the shadow and his eyes moving from one corner of the low structure to the other.

Ever so slowly, as though it hated to leave the landscape and Fargo totally unbaked, the sun lowered and the boulder's shadow consumed the sparse space where the big man lay. He breathed easy now, knowing a showdown had to occur before all light was lost. Then he would have the upper hand, and the Bible Boys knew it. Twilight would be his most dangerous period, so he steeled himself to be ready for it while he watched and listened more keenly than ever for their movement.

When darkness settled over the area and the Bible Boys had not made their move as he expected, he reasoned they were more cowardly than he imagined, then changed his mind. Under cover of darkness, he thought, they may have managed to silently move up.

They're close now, he thought, damn close, and have

their weapons and eyes fixed on the top and both ends of this boulder.

Fargo wrestled with making a decision, but not for long, for any second now they could pounce from three directions. He might be quick enough to get two, but he wondered about downing the third. Drawing his knees up under him, he dug the toes of his boots into the ground. He tensed his muscles to launch him out and away from the stone-and-log sanctuary. Much as he hated the thought, he would have to sacrifice the Sharps to them. He took a deep relaxing breath, exhaled, and pitched the Sharps well behind him, then sprang for the front corner of the trading post at the same time.

A barrage of gunshots ruptured the silence. The bullets tore into the parched earth all around the Sharps. Fargo dived for the corner and rolled around it to safety.

He moved quickly to the far front corner to get in position to challenge them after they discovered the Sharps and that he was no longer at the boulder. They would have no choice then except to make a run for their horses.

He raised the Colt and peered around the corner. Two slugs instantly slammed into the log by his head and showered his face and eyes with splinters. Before he could recover and return fire, he heard hoofbeats pounding away into the night, heading for the foothills. He shot at them anyhow until the Colt fell silent.

Walking to Dugan's front door, he reloaded and whistled for the Ovaro. Elmer Dugan, followed by Little Feather, stepped outside. Both peeled ropes from their arms and legs.

"What the hell's going on out here?" Elmer's whiskey voice demanded. "You okay, Fargo? That is you, ain't it?"

"Yeah, it's me, all right, you old buzzard. Where were you when I needed you?"

"Goddamn, big man like you can't handle five pieces of shit the likes of that bunch?"

"Well, how'd you two manage to tie and gag each other up so good? At least I left two of them for you to bury . . . or leave for the wolves. They're out there among the trees somewhere."

"Yeah, well, me and my woman, we don't bury shit. We'll let the wolves enjoy 'em. Two of 'em busted in and caught us still asleep. After looking around, they said they were gonna let us live. Live, hell. Shit, they tied us up, gagged us, and put blindfolds on us. That goddamn blindfold was the worst part. You going after the other three?"

"Thought I might. No sense leaving a job unfinished."

"Don't go, Fargo," Little Feather cautioned. He Sapa is not for white people. You stay, let my people kill those men. I will fix you a good stew. Will you stay, Fargo?"

"Yeah, Little Feather, I know you make good stew, but I have to go after them or they'll come back and keep killing folks. They don't know their way around in there, nobody does, especially in the dark. I'll catch up to them before they can go very far, then I'll kill them and leave them to rot under the sun."

"Don't go, Fargo," she repeated. "Little Feather says don't go, spirits say do not go. You listen, Fargo. There will be bad trouble if you go."

"She's right," Dugan agreed. "Men go in there and never come back. I'd think twice if I was you. Besides, in case you don't know it, the Sioux are on the move in there, going somewhere to hold council and give the sun dance. Them hills are plumb crawling with red people. They'll hear those three and murder 'em on the spot, no how-comes or what-fors asked."

Fargo answered their warnings by getting in the saddle.

"Thanks for the concern," he said, and rode to retrieve the Sharps before angling the pinto toward the foothills.

The hills soon became a thick tangle of scrub oaks entwined with young pine and elm, all competing for sunlight and moisture to survive. Fargo made slow progress as he rode lengthy east-west switchbacks to pick up their trail north. After he spent a few hours with no success in the pitch-black woods, a waxing three-quarter moon rose high enough for the sun's reflected rays to beam down and penetrate the forest's green canopy. The Trailsman quickened the Ovaro's pace and kept his eyes searching in the dappled soft light for signs.

Midway in a switchback on the downside of yet another pine-infested hill, his vigilance paid off. He reined the pinto to a halt, dismounted to take a closer look at the shod hoofprints. He counted three sets, heading north. Encouraged, he returned to the saddle and added the Ovaro's hoofprints to the clear trail he followed.

An hour of easy tracking passed before the prints entered a heavily wooded, rocky canyon and became erratic, difficult to follow, especially when the Bible Boys rode into a stream but did not come out on the other side. Fargo had to decide which way to go. He chose upstream and scanned both banks as he went. Not more than ten minutes elapsed before he saw where they left the stream and headed toward the smoke he now smelled.

That could mean only one of two things, both bad: either the idiots had built a fire or they were heading straight into an Indian village. Either way they were good as dead.

Fargo followed his nose. The smoke soon became so thick that it alarmed him. He urged the pinto forward faster. Within minutes he rounded a bend only to see the glow from a fire too large for warming or cooking. He stayed on the left bank so the moist soil would mask any sounds the horse's hooves made during his approach to the source of the glow and smoke.

Nearing the danger point, he turned and guided the pinto into a stand of white birch, where he halted. In the clearing before him burned and smoldered the remains of five tepees. Several scalps of long hair, not all black, and eagle feathers tied to the uppermost tips of the burning tepee poles fluttered in the updraft.

He saw no Indians or any ponies, neither of which surprised him. He knew the Sioux never left their wounded or dead behind, and to leave a horse behind was even more unthinkable. There was no question in his mind about it: the fools had successfully carried out the plan he overheard them make earlier while Matt pissed in the creek.

Fargo began riding an arc to circle the encampment and pick up the Bible Boys' trail. If they followed through as stated and took females for their subsequent pleasure, then he'd find them soon enough, for their progress would be extremely slow.

While scanning the ground halfway around the encampment a lance arced in from out of the dark. Its big, sharp point stabbed into the ground less than a yard in front of the Ovaro.

Fargo instantly reined the horse to a halt and focused his eyes on the lance and the many scalps tied to its shaft. He knew better than to touch either the Colt or Sharps, or to wheel and make a run for it. The lance meant arrows or rifles, probably both, were aimed at his heart. It also meant he was to throw down his weapons and dismount. Fargo did both.

Two warriors wielding carbines stepped from a growth of chokecherry bushes and came to stand a few paces in front of him. Both men's angry facial expressions and their nervous body languages clearly indicated to Fargo that he would soon depart from this world. He raised his right arm, bent the elbow, and turned his palm to them so they could see he wasn't armed. In Lakota he said, "*Hau, mi kolas.*" He hoped to hell they would, indeed, be friends.

The two warriors visibly relaxed but maintained their distance. Fargo knew not to extend either hand in friendly gesture or he would be shot instantly. Neither did he close the gap separating them. He heard one of the warriors call to those hidden in the darkness and tell them to come forward, that it was only this one white man. They appeared as though by magic and encircled him with their bows and arrows and carbines at the ready.

An elder, white-haired and tired-looking, came to stand between the two warriors. Before the old man could speak, the Trailsman told him in his own language, "Grandfather, I come in peace. My name is Skye Fargo. I am from far away. The white men who did this are also my enemies, Grandfather. They are the enemies of many white men. They are bad humans, Grandfather, lower than our relatives who wriggle on our Mother Earth. Grandfather, I have come to kill them, not to harm you or your people. Believe I speak the truth. I know this land is sacred, forbidden to the white man, but, Grandfather, I had to come or they will go on killing."

The old man grunted, sat, and motioned for the others to do likewise. After a moment of silence, he said, "It is good you speak Lakota, white man, and show respect for my people and our sacred land. This is the only reason you are not dead."

Fargo replied, "Thank you, Grandfather. Did they kill any of your people?"

"Yes, Skye Fargo, they killed six of the people. Three old men and one woman who could not run fast enough to escape. They cut the pony guard's throat and struck without any warning. Each took a young woman when they rode off in that direction." He faced east and puckered his lips.

Fargo felt ashamed, not of his race, but what it was doing to these people. "So reckless," he muttered, then strengthened his voice when he said, "Grandfather, all I can do is apologize for this horrible incident, which was so unnecessary. Not all of my white brothers are like these men. Again, I come here in peace. Will you allow me to leave? I must find the murderers."

The old man thought while drawing an elongated circle in the soil before him. Finally, he looked up at Fargo. "Yes, Skye Fargo, you can leave."

Pausing, he dragged a finger across the drawing, then continued, "What you see that I have put in the earth is our sacred Black Hills. We are here," he said, and placed a fingertip in the lower extremity of the drawing. "Do not go past the line I have made. We are Miniconju Lakota. All of the Lakota people—and the Dakota and Nakota as well—are allies, white man. All of our allies are going to a certain most sacred place. We cannot take the time to hunt down and kill these insane humans. You are free to kill them for us, but do not go past the line I drew or I will not be able to speak up for you."

"I understand, Grandfather," Fargo replied. "When I catch up to these wild white men, I will slaughter them. If the women they carried away are still alive, I will bring them back to you."

"And if they are dead?" the old man asked.

"Then I will release their souls to the Great Spirit, Grandfather."

The old man stiffened slightly as his eyes showed his surprise. "You know this sacred rite, Skye Fargo?"

"I'm aware of it, Grandfather. My brothers, the Two Kettles, have told me."

The old man turned at the waist and spoke to a woman in the circle behind him. She immediately left her position in the circle and ran to the remains of the tepees and began poking through the debris. They sat in silence until she returned and handed the old man several buckskin pouches, each of which was tied to long loops of buckskin thongs.

When the old man sorted them out, Fargo saw three identical pouches. The old man handed them to him, saying, "If our women are dead, take clippings of a fingernail or toenail from each woman and some of her hair. Place these things in a pouch. Do the same for her sisters. Keep the pouches in a safe place, Fargo, for they hold the woman's soul. Give the pouches to the first Lakota you see. Tell him what I have told you and tell him when you found the women. Explain to him that you found the women during the time of our great council at Bear Butte. He will know what to do with their souls. Understand?"

Fargo nodded, hung the thongs around his neck, and moved to stand, but the old man gestured for him to remain seated. Fargo watched him turn his head and nod.

Within seconds a woman stepped forward and handed the old man a length of freshly picked sage, from which he stripped the tender aromatic leaves, then rolled them into a ball. The Trailsman watched as the old man purified his hands. Now the elder could receive the pipe.

As one of the warriors sitting beside him crumbled dry grass and laid it on the ground, the woman gave Fargo a strand of sage. In that instant he knew the elder would share the pipe with him, a great honor, an act of peace, for the pipe was central to their spiritual beliefs.

Fargo rolled the tender leaves in his palms as the elder had done.

The woman struck two pieces of flint at the ball of grass, and fire blossomed. The other warrior put the tip of a twig to the blaze and lit it, then held it to the opening of the pipe bowl.

The old man drew deeply on the long stem's mouthpiece, then symbolically washed his head and face in the cloud of smoke he exhaled, then uttered, *"Me-tock-we-oh-seh,"* and passed the pipe to Fargo.

The big man gripped the warm bowl firmly, brought the end of the pipe stem to his mouth, then inhaled deeply. Exhaling the sacred smoke, he too washed his face and head symbolically. But Fargo spoke in English, rather than in Lakota, when saying the same closing spiritual comment as the old man had to seal the agreement made with the Miniconju, "All my relations."

The old man motioned for him to pass the pipe to the warrior on his right.

Fargo watched the pipe pass sunwise from one set of waiting, sage-purified hands to another. As each took his turn, the others maintained reverent silence, sat motionless. When the sacred tobacco had been smoked out, the pipe was returned to the old man. He took it apart, blew the residue from both bowl and stem, pronounced all my relations in his language, then looked at Fargo and smiled for the first time when he said, *"Lee-lah wash-tay."*

The Trailsman nodded, answered, "Yes, Grandfather, very good."

When the old man stood, so did the others.

Fargo went to the Ovaro held in wait by two youngsters. He fluffed each boy's hair, smiled, gave each a wink, then climbed onto the saddle.

The original two warriors handed him his weapons, then stood back. One said, "You are our brother and our friend, white man. We will not harm you because of this. But while we respect our headman's wisdom, Fargo, he did not say this is the end of the matter. This story will be told many times around fires at the great council and sun dance. My warrior brothers and I will ride after the sun dance. We will punish many white people for what these three have done."

Fargo believed they would do exactly that. He nodded to them, turned the Ovaro eastward, and rode away.

4

Fargo picked up the Bible Boys' trail slightly north and east on the perimeter of the Miniconju's encampment. He followed it easily until the hoofprints entered the stream. He halted to dismount and refill his canteen while the stallion drank from the cool stream. Again he had to make a choice of which way to search.

Again he chose upstream and rode in the shallow water as he watched both banks. After about a mile he concluded he'd been wrong. He turned back and rode on the left bank while returning to where they had taken to the stream. Less than a hundred yards south he saw the shod hoofprints on the right bank.

Almost immediately the prints turned and headed in a southwesterly direction. Fargo followed them out of the walled canyon, then lost sight of their path when it ended abruptly in a thicket of undergrowth barely visible in the heavy shadows.

After working his way through the dense growth and out of the dark shadows, he executed a wide circle to find their signs but found none. That meant they had changed direction while in the shadowy area. He paused to think and decided that inasmuch as they were obviously heading in a more southerly direction than eastern or western, they were probably returning to the main artery used by settlers going west. "They mentioned sacking Hubbard's Crossing," he muttered in thought.

Fargo abandoned his night search. He rode for the trading post.

Shortly before breaking out into the foothills, he passed a large outcrop of jagged rocks surrounded by bur oak, elm, and sapling pine. As he guided the Ovaro between junipers, he heard snarls from within the rocky formation and reined the pinto to a halt. Drawing the Colt, he decided to go check.

He approached cautiously, keeping the horse at a slow walk. The snarls and guttural growls became louder. He now knew they were made by wolves arguing over a nocturnal meal. Before riding into the rocks, he fired the Colt.

Several dark forms fled from the outcrop and vanished into the dense shadows. He knew the animals hadn't gone very far. They were watching him, waiting for him to leave so they could return to feed.

He eased the Ovaro around the outer edges of the crag and looked in. The stench of shit was overpowering. Even in the murky shadows he recognized the wolves had been feeding on human flesh. At least two mutilated bodies lay in the tight space. He fired another shot to intimidate the wolves, then eased from the saddle and went in for a better look.

He recognized them immediately as being two of the Miniconju women. What was left of them. Both were nude. They'd been hacked on. The wolves had favored their rumps and thighs. Bowels lay open, the source of the nauseating smell. Fargo slipped his neckerchief up over his nose and began pulling the women's remains out of the rocks.

In the moonlight he saw their throats had been slashed

and their bodies mutilated before the wolves had found them. Fargo shook his head, turned, and began using his mighty strength to bend and break several pine saplings to make into a travois for hauling the bodies to Dugan's place.

After attaching the travois to the Ovaro, he dragged the two mangled corpses by the ankles and placed them side by side on the patch frame he'd made from dead tree branches. As he was tying the bodies down, he heard a low moan that he knew no wolf made, and he paused. Kicking his eyes up, he drew the Colt and fell to the left, ready to aim and fire.

From his prone position at the rocks, he glanced about the area and saw no movement. He was ready to believe his wild-creature hearing had played a trick on him when he heard the low sound again. This time there was no mistake about where it came from or what made it. His vision lifted and focused on the branches of one of the elms. He stood and moved to stand under the tree and look up into its limbs and leaves.

She lay astraddle a limb where it grew out of the trunk, both legs and arms hanging lifeless, her silhouette camouflaged by the shape of the tree itself and in the shadows of it. Fargo holstered the Colt and prepared to climb up and get her. In that instant she moved, lost all balance, and fell from the limb. He jumped back and caught her just before she hit the ground.

He carried the nude woman out into the moonlight and gently laid her faceup on a patch of cool grass. Although she'd been beaten and stabbed, he saw why they had taken her in preference to others.

The young woman's body was long, slim, and work-firm, and her face was most beautiful, especially her wide mouth and full lips. Bruises showed on her shoulders and left cheek. She'd been stabbed in the left shoulder and cut above her navel and on the right forearm. None appeared too serious. He felt over her head and found the big lump where she had been hit.

Fargo rolled her onto one side and looked at her back. He found a bruise near her right shoulder blade. Other than that, all he saw were a pair of small but nicely rounded cheeks. The big man put her on her back, then went to the travois and completed tying down her dead sisters.

He placed his bedroll on the upper end of the platform, as far away from the two mangled bodies as possible. Then he fetched the injured young woman and put her in the fetal position on the bedroll, secured her in place, mounted, and rode south for the foothills.

At first light Elmer Dugan's trading post came into the big man's view. He negotiated the Ovaro down through the low spots in the hills and broke out onto flat grassy land well behind the corral. Smoke rising from the chimney promised that Little Feather, at least, was up and stirring about.

Dugan appeared at the left front corner holding a revolver. Fargo chuckled when he saw how absurd the garrulous man looked. Dugan was dressed only in baggy red long johns with the back flap undone and hanging down to his knees, but wearing his boots and wide-brim black hat with two eagle feathers stuck in its band.

"Whatcha towing?" Dugan asked as he stepped farther away from the low structure to have a better look.

"Miniconju," Fargo answered. "Two dead, one barely breathing."

Dugan followed alongside the travois when Fargo got to him and went around to the front entrance. "Goddamn, Fargo, I know you ain't one to butcher females. Was it them?"

"Yep, one and same," he replied, and dismounted.

Coming to stand next to Elmer, he added, "What they didn't do, wolves did." Releasing the rope that held the young unconscious woman down in place, he commented, "This one fell out of an elm. You lift her by the ankles and I'll take the arms."

Dugan moved to his side of the travois and grabbed her ankles. Together they gently lifted her off the bedroll and carried the woman into the trading post.

Spying Little Feather standing at the cook stove, Fargo said, " 'Morning, Little Feather. Got a job for you."

The huge rolly-polly woman muttered, "Unh," and looked over her right broad shoulder. She went back to her cooking.

Fargo swung the woman's body around and over the bed and lowered her head onto a torn pillow.

Gazing up and down her body, Dugan said, "Ain't nothing we can do for her 'cept watch." Nodding toward the door, he added, "Let's go get rid of the others before this place is so stunk up we'll have to move. My woman will see to this'n in a minute. Little Feather, put the coffee on. Fargo looks like he could use some."

They went out front to discuss where and how to bury the bodies. Dugan was for digging a hole and dropping them down it. "What the hell," he began offhandedly, "when you're dead, you're dead and don't give a big damn."

Little Feather's enormous bulk instantly filled the doorway. "Do not dig holes for Indians, Dugan." Without further explanation, she turned and disappeared inside.

Fargo agreed with her and suggested, "We'll go just far enough into the foothills so settlers passing this way can't see the scaffold."

Dugan's face screwed up and he actually removed his hat to rub a hand over his head and face when he complained, "Scaffold? C'mon, Fargo, not a damn scaffold. Not in this heat. Why—"

Little Feather's voice boomed from within. "Dugan, shut up. Help Fargo make a scaffold. Now!"

Fargo looked at the little guy and shrugged.

"Awright," Elmer mumbled in capitulation, "let's go and get it over with before somebody drops by to buy something for the kiddies back East."

"You wish," Fargo said through a smug grin, and mounted up. He'd often wondered why Elmer Dugan continued to operate a trading post. He'd never seen the man sell or trade anything, but only buy. Dugan was a soft touch in spite of his outward appearance and callous speech, as evidenced by the waist-high piles of stuff on the floor. All walls of the log building were filled with the strangest of items. More hung from the rafters.

Dugan came behind him but angled off to the woodpile to get his ax. Grabbing it up, he sauntered to the corral to get a pick and shovel. Fargo proceeded into the foothills and stopped at a low place large enough for the scaffold. Elmer arrived puffing and huffing and plopped down on the ground to catch his wind.

"You never did say what happened," Dugan uttered between gasps. "Before you found 'em, I mean. Like, how'd you know they be Miniconju? Naked Indian women all look the same, cain't tell one band from another." He held the ax handle out for Fargo to take.

Fargo said nothing until he'd put the first cut in a lodgepole pine. "They caught a bunch of Miniconju sleeping, murdered six, torched the settlement, took souvenirs and these three." While felling the required number of lodgepoles, he told Elmer the rest of the story.

Elmer used Fargo's knife to pick the soft bark away from the trimmed poles and, peeling one, said, "Promised to raise hell with us, huh? They mean it, big man. Them Sioux don't make idle threats."

Fargo took the knife from him and began stripping

bark off another pole. "So, you going to stay put, El-mer? Reckon they'd leave you alone, seeing how's Little Feather's Sioux?"

Elmer burst out laughing and replied, "Shit, they'd take my scalp without thinking twice. Little Feather hold-ing on to me wouldn't make no difference. No, I ain't staying put. I'm loading up and getting the hell outta here. High time I left anyhow. I got a fortune in that cabin and it ain't worth a penny out here. Mebbe I'll take Little Feather to Saint Louis and let her see how fancy white folks live."

They had made the burial rack, attached it to the top parts of the poles, and were in the process of standing the scaffold upright when Little Feather appeared, bear-ing two folded Indian blankets. She sat in the shade of a hill and watched while they heaved it up and worked the bottoms of the four poles down into the holes Dugan had dug. Only then did she comment. *"Wash-tay. Lee-lah wash-tay.* Fargo does good work."

Elmer turned to her and showed her his palms. "Fargo, hell," he squalled. "See these hands, woman? They did it while Fargo watched."

"Bullshit," she answered, and said no more.

Fargo spread the colorful blankets side by side on the ground, then laid the dead faceup on them and moved to fold the ends up over them. Little Feather stopped him with a hoarse grunt that clearly meant he wasn't doing something correct. He paused and looked at her. She glanced to the sunny side of a low rise behind him, puck-ered her lips toward the sage covering the rise, and said, "Wait. Dugan, go pick some sage to put in blankets."

Elmer sighed, said it was getting hot, and stomped over into the sage and plucked an armful. Fargo relieved him of it and divided the bundle onto and around the women. As he did, the buckskin pouches swung on their thongs and caught his eye. He removed two of them from around his neck, placed them on the edge of one blanket, and opened the pouches.

He drew his knife again from its sheath tied to the calf of his left leg, then knelt by one of the dead women to take a length of her hair.

Little Feather stopped him with another grunt.

He sat back on his heels and looked at her. Holding the knife out he said, "You do it, Little Feather."

She heaved her massive bulk from the ground with surprising ease, came to take his knife. She handed hair, fingernail, and toenail clippings to Fargo as she cut them. When he had them in their proper pouches and tied each snugly, he handed them to her, but she refused to touch them, saying, "No, Fargo, you keep them. Little Feather is a white man's woman now. I do not go back to my people. You must give these to a Lakota woman. She keeps the four seasons. She knows what to do."

Fargo draped the thongs around his neck, then proceeded to bundle the women for burial. That part completed, he lifted Elmer onto his shoulders and hoisted him onto the platform, then pressed each bundled woman up over his head and into Dugan's waiting arms. Dugan arranged them side by side, their eyes facing their ancestors across the great river in the south. Fargo helped him down and they looked at Little Feather.

She rose when they removed their hats, came forward, and took one of the eagle feathers from Dugan's hat band, turned, and held it up toward the west. They listened to her pray to that spirit to give the dead women's souls a safe journey to the spirit world. As she turned to each of the other three directions and repeated the prayer to those spirits, Dugan and Fargo also turned.

Then she lifted her eyes and the eagle feather skyward, offered the same prayer to the Great Spirit, then looked down, touched the tip of the feather to the ground at her feet, and repeated the prayer to Mother Earth, Maka Ina, after which she uttered, *"Me-tock-wi-oh-seh,"* then handed the feather to Dugan. There was nothing more to be done. They turned and went back to the trading post.

Fargo saw Little Feather had bathed the unconscious young female and tended to her wounds but left her stretched out naked and uncovered. The huge woman saw his frown and explained, "Too hot for cover. She's nice-looking, yes, Fargo?"

"Yes, she is beautiful," Fargo agreed.

"Fargo want?" Elmer chuckled.

Little Feather backhanded him into a pile of buffalo robes. When she turned to give Fargo a hard look, he immediately lost any interest in the woman's fine copper-colored body. The big man threw his hands up as he backed out of Little Feather's striking distance. That's when the girl moaned and stirred awake.

Her eyes opened slowly at first, then flared when she saw Fargo and Dugan's bearded faces. Without rising she cut her eyes about the room. Her concerned gaze stopped to briefly consider Little Feather, then looked past Elmer's grin and made eye contact with Fargo. He saw her muscles tense an instant before she vaulted off the bed and ran for the doorway.

Fargo's left arm shot out, hooked her by the slim waist, and jerked her off her feet. She screamed and clawed at his face as he turned her back to press against his chest and fling her back onto the bed.

Dugan stepped into the doorway to prevent her escape. It was well that he did, because she bounced off the far side of the bed and started darting around the room, looking for a way out.

Fargo let her get used to the idea that while she was trapped, none of them were going to hurt her. When her initial panic waned somewhat, he spoke to her in her language. "Last night you fell from a tree into my arms. I brought you here. We are your friends. What is your name, girl?"

Her eyes bounced from his to Dugan, to Little Feather, and back to him. "Where am I?" she asked. "Where are my people?"

Little Feather spoke Lakota to her. "This is my tepee." Puckering at Dugan, she said, "He is my man. You are safe here. Are you hungry? I have made hot soup."

"No," she replied. "Where are my people?"

Fargo answered, "They have left for the great council. I told your headman I would look for you and the other two women the white butchers took."

Again she cut sharp glances about the room, obviously looking for her sisters. "Where—"

Little Feather interrupted. "Gone. They journey to the Spirit World." She picked up one of her dresses and pitched it to the young woman. "Cover yourself with it, then sit to eat my soup while we talk long."

The young woman slipped the dress's extra-wide hem over her head. Before she could catch the extra-wide collar, the dress fell down her body and onto the floor. She stooped and picked it up. This time she was careful to draw the collar string tightly around her shoulders to prevent the garment from falling.

Dugan looked at Little Feather. "Look at that, will ya? Woman, I've been telling you that you've gotta lose weight." He ducked in time to keep from getting hit with the pot Little Feather flung at him.

"Get a short piece of rope, Elmer," Fargo said. "Or something she can use for a belt, otherwise she'll keep stepping out of that dress." When Little Feather glowered at him, he hurried to add, "No offense, Little Feather, no offense intended."

Dugan produced a wide red belt from one of the many piles and tossed it to the woman. She pulled it around her waist and buckled it. Looking up, she nodded and began a smile that she quickly checked. Fargo gestured they sit at the kitchen table and she reluctantly left her safe position to sit in the chair facing Fargo.

He saw her looking at the three pouches hanging on his chest. He spoke while pulling the thongs over his head and handing the pouches to her. "The headman gave them to me and instructed me on what to do should I find any of you dead. He asked me to give them to any Lakota. He or she would know what to do. So, girl, you take them."

She hung them around her neck without comment, then accepted Little Feather's hot soup when Dugan's woman placed a bowl of it before her. While partaking of the vegetable soup, the girl asked what was going to happen now and how would she return to her people.

Fargo answered, "First tell us how you escaped being killed like your two sisters. I found all three of you in about the same place."

They watched her eyes close as she obviously relived the nightmare, saying, "We were terrified. Everyone was. The whole encampment. Those men were on us before anyone knew what was happening. At first we thought they were Blackfeet or Cheyenne who had attacked to steal women and ponies. Then we saw it was white men. They were running everywhere, shooting and throwing fire inside the tepees. I thought there were a lot of men, maybe your army soldiers, but there were only three. They were so mean to us. We fought them, but they were too strong. They rode fast, like crazy people. I don't know how far they took us, or where, before they stopped, but it was a long way . . . in some rocks.

"The smallest one separated me from the others and

beat me all the way to where he took and shoved me onto the ground. I could hear Two Fawns and Pretty Water screaming for them not to hurt them. I heard those horrible white men hitting them while they laughed and tore their dresses off, just like mine was doing to me over in dark shadows. I never saw his face.

"I never saw any of their faces. He cut my dress off with his knife, then put his hands on my breasts and pulled on them. Oh, it hurt. It hurt real bad. He didn't care. I thought he'd get on top of me and, and, and hurt me, but he didn't. He pulled my legs apart, and, and, and he used his mouth on me.

"When he finished, he tried to stab me in the heart, but I saw the knife coming down and moved out of its way. The blade missed my heart and went in my shoulder. He stood and kicked me, then left me for dead. I lay still, holding my breath, forcing myself to keep quiet, and hoped he wouldn't come back.

"I listened to them get on their horses. They were laughing and yelling when they rode away. It was quiet over at those rocks. Real quiet. After waiting to make sure they were gone and weren't coming back, I crawled over to the rocks. Two Fawns and Pretty Water, they were . . . they had been—"

Fargo broke into her nightmare, knowing she was again seeing what she had seen, what he had found. "Then the wolves came?"

She nodded and made a face. "Yes. I heard a growl and looked behind me. About eight of them were standing, watching from the trees. I yelled at them and threw a rock, but I knew they wouldn't run away. They had smelled the blood. My head was dizzy and I started getting numb all over.

"Sometimes I could see and sometimes I was blind. I had to get away from them even if it meant leaving Two

Fawns and Pretty Water for them. I cried for them, for what had happened and for what I knew was going to happen. I forced myself to stand, then staggered toward a tree. I fell down several times, and one of the wolves rushed in and snapped at me each time.

"I got up and kept going. I knew I would be safe if I could get to the tree. The last thing I remember is hugging my arms around the trunk, then seeing your faces when my eyes opened again."

They watched her lift the rim of the soup bowl to her mouth. As she sipped the steaming broth, Fargo said, "If you feel up to riding, I'll take you to a place where I have to meet with people, white people. I'll see to it somebody takes you north to your people at the great council."

The young woman's eyes peered over the top of the bowl and moved across his powerful chest and muscular arms. She made a slight nod as she looked up into his lake-blue eyes.

Dugan said, "Those three sons of bitches are gonna bring the whole Sioux nation down on us. Shit!" Glancing at Little Feather's somber face, he added, "Soon's Fargo and the girl leave, you go pull the Owensboro 'round front. We'll start loading up to clear out till this mess blows over."

"Unh," the huge woman replied. "You pull the wagon. I will load. Take me Saint Louis. We can trade."

"You're the boss," Dugan agreed. He pushed back from the table to obey.

Fargo stood, followed him outside, and whistled for the Ovaro. As the horse trotted around the west corner, the girl appeared at Fargo's side. "I will ride with you on this big horse, big man?"

He knew she was accustomed to walking while the men rode, so her question was more of a wonderment than a plea. "Yes," he answered, "in front of me."

He mounted up, then reached and took her hand. When he yanked her up, she sprung gracefully, her long slim left leg raised high to clear the horse's powerful withers and lit between him and the saddle horn. He felt her small rump cram against his spread thighs, then squirm to find a comfortable spot away from the hard horn nuzzling her midnight patch. Nodding to Little Feather, he put the Ovaro in a walk and headed east into the hot yellow sun. "It's never going to rain again," he muttered.

"Talk Lakota," she complained. "Where are you taking me?"

"To a place called Gully Town. Know it?"

"Yes. I was there one time many moons ago. My father and his warriors went there to see how white people live. They took me and Pretty Water with them so we could learn too."

"And? What did you learn? By the way, you never told us your name. You do have a name?"

"Certainly. Like all my people, I have three names, but I will tell you only one, my everyday name. They call me Sings Loud Woman."

"Very pretty. Will you sing for me?"

"No," she replied flatly. He waited for her to explain. When she didn't, he didn't press for a reason. After about a quarter-mile, she commented, "Your people live funny. They act strange. Your women wear war paint and have big eyes. The men have hair on their faces" —she glanced over her shoulder at his beard—"like you. I was afraid of them. So was Pretty Water. They stared at us. Some winked and smiled. What does that mean, wink and smile? My father didn't know. One of the men handed my father pieces of round silver and looked at Pretty Water. The man made his head go up and down. My father didn't know what that meant either, so he gave the silver back to the white man. That man became angry."

"Well, girl, you might as well know so you'll know what to do if it ever happens again. That white man wanted to get between Pretty Water's legs."

She half-turned and stared at him with shocked disbelief flashing in her dark eyes. "Why?"

Fargo's grin was his only answer. He wondered if the Bible Boy had been the first to plow in her garden, albeit with his mouth and tongue. "How young is Sings Loud Woman?" he asked, prepared to hear her reply that she didn't know.

"My mother said I came when the first snow flew. She cut a notch in my cradleboard each time the first snow flew after that. There are ten-and-seven notches."

"Have you slept with a man?"

Again she turned, this time showing a quizzical expression. She answered, "Certainly," then turned to face forward. He felt her rump scrooch against his bunch-up and start squiggling slowly from side to side. Almost immediately her cheeks parted and his husky lump wedged into the crack. Fargo felt her tensing and relaxing her cheek muscles on his protrusion. She commented, "Do I not please you?"

"You most certainly do please me," he sighed, and looked at the sun.

And so they rode, him tall and straight in the saddle and the Indian girl, Sings Loud Woman, leaning against his chest, her often hard, sometimes pillow-soft rear rocking across his pent-up organ in rhythm with the pinto's movements.

Relief came for both of them at sundown when they arrived at the campfire, the smoke from which they'd been watching for over an hour. The cooking fire was next to nine wagons parked in line with the wagon tongues pointing westward. Fargo noted five were the ones he'd seen overturned at Buzzard's Gap. He counted nineteen settlers: four women, eight children, and seven men. He reckoned one of the men would be the wagon master and two of the others his helpers, the other four husbands of the women. The children, he noted, were loud and unruly.

They watched him and the girl ride in. An older man with a weather-beaten face and deeply tanned leathered hands holding a tin cup of steaming coffee stepped beside the Ovaro. Offering the cup up to Fargo, he looked at Sings Loud Woman and said, "Howdy, mister. Name's Roscoe Taylor. Me and my help's taking these folks to Oregon." He looked to Fargo when the big man took the cup from him. "Evening meal's about ready. Beans and rabbit meat Clarence and Emmett plunked. You're welcome to have some of it with us."

Fargo sipped from the brew, then nodded. "Thanks, Mr. Taylor. That rabbit does make my mouth water." In Lakota he asked Sings Loud Woman, "You want some of that rabbit? He said we can eat with them." When she nodded, he handed the empty cup to Taylor and nudged the girl to dismount. Her right leg swept over the horse's neck and she dropped to the ground. Fargo followed. She clung to his gun belt as they went to join the others.

Fargo noticed the children had quietened and gathered closely around their mothers. All eyes were fixed on Sings Loud Woman.

He explained, "I'm taking her back to her people, the Miniconju. She and two others were captured last night by three madmen. Those men are still around, so you want to keep your eyes open."

One of the women handed him a plate of beans with a leg of rabbit. Another handed more of the same to the girl. They sat and began eating.

One of the husbands, a tall lanky fellow with tired eyes, asked, "Being alone out here and going in the wrong direction, you must know this land pretty good."

Fargo nodded.

"That being the case," he continued, "what's it look like for us up ahead? Mr. Taylor says this is Sioux territory and they sometimes turn hostile. Are we in danger"—he glanced at the girl and nodded—"with her in our midst?"

Fargo answered while gnawing on the overcooked leg. "No, not while she's with me. You may have to watch out for the Sioux, but not on account of her." He looked at Taylor. "It's the Bible Boys you have to worry about most."

"Bible Boys?" a pinch-faced woman gasped. "Did you hear that, Hiram? The Bible Boys are way out here."

Hiram asked, "You sure you're not mistaken, mister? We heard they were in Minnesota someplace."

"Might have been," Fargo began, "but they're down here now. Gutted Gully Town the other night. Murdered a bunch of folks and burned half the town to the ground. I caught up with them on down this trail a ways, at Elmer Dugan's trading post." He paused to look at Taylor. "You know the place?"

"Absolutely," Taylor answered quickly. "I've known Elmer for years. He's all ri—"

Fargo stopped him with a sharp nod. "He's okay. When you get to his place, he'll tell you all about what happened. The only good part about it is, I cut the Bible Boys' number from five to three. But I swear those three are the toughest of the lot. Meanest too. So, friend, be careful if you see three riders coming, one on a big dun. My advice is for you to shoot first and ask questions later."

Out the corners of his eyes he noticed the Indian girl flinch. A hard look appeared on her face. Turning to look, he saw a boy of about ten stab her in the back with his hand formed into a make-believe pistol. The kid

77

went, "Bang!" When he did it again, the other children giggled.

Sings Loud Woman jerked her left elbow behind her and knocked the annoying hand away.

The boy yelped, "She hit me, Mama! I didn't do nothing and she just hit me! Ow!"

The kid's mother's eyes narrowed into slits and her lips tightened over her teeth. Without preamble she flung her tin plate aside, then lunged for the girl. Sings Loud Woman fell to her left and grabbed the onrushing heavier woman by the hair and slammed her face into the hard ground. Before anyone could react, the young Indian had the woman bellydown and sat astride her at the waist. She pulled the woman's head back with one fistful of hair, then drove her face into the ground with the other.

Fargo got to them first. He grabbed Sings Loud Woman's slim waist and yanked her off the screaming mother. Sings Loud Woman's body trembled beneath his strong grip, straining to get free to pound the woman unconscious. He lifted her off the ground and clutched her backside to him.

By then everyone had stood and were staring perplexed at them. Taylor cleared his throat and said, "Mister, tell that hellcat of yours we can't have no more of that. We're all peaceable folks, and I don't put up with fighting."

Fargo eyed him coldly as he said, "Then I suggest you tell these people to teach their young good manners and how to behave properly. You saw it, Taylor. The girl was minding her own business. She—"

"Injun whore," the bloody-faced woman growled, and spit on Sings Loud Woman.

With a little help from Fargo, the girl wrenched free of his grip. She leapt with her legs spread apart and clamped them around the woman's waist. Both hit the ground hard. Sings Loud Woman hammered her fist onto the woman's mouth several times, splitting both lips wide open, before Fargo pulled her off.

Taylor said, "Mister, I suggest you two mount up and leave. I'm not putting up with this any longer. Next time I'll have to shoot the bitch."

Fargo tossed the girl onto the saddle, then eased up behind her. Looking down at Taylor, he nudged the Ovaro forward and said, "Well, friend, I'd hate to see you shoot that boy's ma, but I guess you're right, she'd sure deserve it."

He rode until the wagons were out of sight, then stopped and lowered Sings Loud Woman to the ground. He handed the bedroll down to her and in Lakota said, "We will sleep here tonight. Spread it out while I get rid of some of that bad coffee they gave me." He dismounted and walked a distance to relieve himself.

When he returned, he found her lying nude on the bedroll. Even in the dim starlight he saw her dark eyes shining as they watched his. She lay with her long slender arms outstretched and her slim legs parted wide, obviously inviting him to take her, ready to enfold the limbs around his body and not let go until he lay limp, breathing relaxed.

As he unbuckled and shed his clothes beside the bedroll, his gaze moved from her pretty face to her youthful breasts. He did not miss seeing her large nipples, which were punching heavenward, nor her flat belly, which rose and fell in cadence with her inner eagerness. Continuing his downward survey of the young beauty, he focused on the huge lush growth of glistening pitch-black hair that covered her Venus mound and hid the vertical lips of her lower wonder.

He heard her gasp when she saw him fully naked. As

he knelt, her left hand raised and her long fingers coiled around his long staff. She stroked it twice. Her breathing quickened as he watched her eyes, now wide and filled with excitement, glance about his chest, shoulders, and neck.

She whispered, "Yours is a beautiful body, white man, all muscle. I want to feel it crush on mine." She pulled on his organ.

Fargo bent and took her right nipple between his lips, rolled it around them tightly, then sucked in the wide circle of dark areolae and most of the supple mound of flesh. She moaned and started squirming, drawing her legs inward, then back out, teasing her lower lips to moisten and swell, to dilate for the massiveness enlarging in her left hand.

She moved his right hand down and grasped it between her thighs, raised her buttocks, and squirmed to fit his middle finger into the moist sheath. He slid the finger into her hot nook and rubbed it up and down, slickening the swollen opening with her own secretion, preparing it for the stretching. The girl writhed and gulped, emitted a series of quick gasps, and moaned, "My other breast . . . take it too, big man. Push deeper down there. Deeper, please. Oh, yes, that's good. I am floating in the stars."

He sucked the other nipple and breast, worked a second finger into the opening, circled them around the soft walls, circled wider and wider until she groaned, "My insides are on fire. I'm having visions, big man . . . the sky is opening up. It's beautiful. Oh, that feels good. I want more."

He felt her hands on the sides of his face. She drew his lips and mouth from the breast. Breathing hard and hot, she rubbed her palms over his powerful chest twice, then pushed him backward onto the ground and impaled her head on his towering manliness.

As she sucked downward, her head twisted from side to side, forcing her hot mouth and soft throat to be gorged with his hardness. From within the long black mane shielding her savoring, he heard whimpers of enchantment mixed with gurgles of strangulation. Within moments her encircling hot tongue brought him to the brink of exploding. He pulled her head back and she gasped hard for breath. When Fargo pushed her onto her back, she opened her thighs to accept him. He knelt between them, took a firm buttock cheek in each hand, and lifted her groin. She reached down, grasped his throbbing organ with both hands, and shrieked as she fed the swollen crown into her begging nook.

Fargo, poised to make deep penetration, hesitated for the inner tissue to relax and minimize the pain from additional widening. During the pause, he thrust her ass upward and shoved. "Aaeeiiii," she screamed as her tight passageway swallowed his member. Fargo felt her long legs lock around his hard waist, then draw tight. She pumped, moaning, "My insides are on fire . . ."

He fused her slippery crotch to his and they gyrated together, he clockwise, she counterclockwise. She poked a nipple and its breast back between his lips, then pushed her chest until he had both fully consumed in his mouth. Her hands gripped the cheeks of his ass. He felt her fingernails raking them furiously while she continued to grunt and groan and gasp her enthrallment. "Yes, yes, big man . . . more, big man . . . make it go deeper . . . oh, oh, please . . . now, that's it. Aaeeiiii!"

With her climax came a fierce contraction of her inner walls, and he flooded her deepest recesses. She unlocked her legs and raked his torso with her knees and clawed his back, screaming, "Aaeeiiii . . . aaeeiiii, I'm on fire."

Fargo flinched, opened his eyes, and looked at her when she started singing loudly to the stars overhead.

When she finished the song of love and happiness, she looked at him and smiled. "I don't want to go back to my people," she whispered. "I want to stay with Bull Buffalo-Prick Man."

He rolled off and lay beside her. Placing her head into the crook of his left shoulder, she teased his left nipple with her tongue. He said, "It would never do, you with me, Hellcat Woman. Tempted though I am to let you."

She bit the nipple and said, "Did I please you? No Miniconju man will have me now. Only you can fill me now."

Fargo chuckled. "By morning it will be back to normal. Go to sleep, Sings Loud Woman. When you awake, you'll find I'm right."

She answered by grasping his limpness and massaged it till it stood erect and jerking, then she swung her firm body on top of his. She fell asleep holding its sturdiness between her thighs at the matted black convergence.

The big man looked at her peaceful face. She had been beaten, hauled off, beaten again, and stabbed. She had listened to her sisters beg for their lives only to be savagely murdered and left for the wolves to devour. Then she'd got on a horse with a complete stranger—a white man no less—and rode away with him on the strength of his word that he would return her to her people. She'd had to fight a woman on the way. After all of that, she still had the energy to bed the big man.

But, then, it came as no surprise to the Trailsman. He knew Indian women, especially Sioux women, were accustomed to rough treatment. Theirs was a hard life.

Only the strong survived.

5

The soft sounds from a crackling fire awoke the Trails-man. Cutting his eyes toward the tiny flames, he saw Sings Loud Woman sitting cross-legged. She had dressed and sat facing him from the far side of the small fire. He glanced to the still-dull gray eastern horizon, then turned back to her.

She smiled and uncrossed her legs. Bending them at the knees, she opened them and drew the hem of Little Feather's dress up to her slim waist. Rubbing fingers over her pubic hair, she said, "You were wrong, big man. It still begs for you. It's swollen and sore from all the stretching. It hurts to walk. But I've never felt so wonderful in all my life. Everything is so beautiful." With the free hand she laid another stick on the fire and increased her smile.

He said, "There's jerky in the left saddlebag. We'll eat, then be on our way."

He watched her stand, stretch and yawn, then step to the saddlebags and get the jerky. She sat beside him, touching his waist with one knee. She handed him a length of the dried meat, saying, "I slept like a baby with a full stomach. Content." She bent her lips to his and kissed him for the first time. When he cupped her left breast in his hand, she flinched and mewed, "Easy, big man. I'm sore there also. In a good way, though. Your hands feel good touching me, so don't stop. Be gentle . . . at first."

Fargo love-bit her lower lip, patted her hip, and rose. He walked a short distance before turning his back to the firelight to relieve himself on a clump of buffalo grass. He noted that Sings Loud Woman wasn't the only one who had extra-tender body parts this morning; he too was a mite sore. Shaking it, he muttered to the last glimmering stars, "I'll give it a couple of days' rest. Be good as new." He bit a hunk from the jerky and chewed it on the way back to the fire.

As he saddled the Ovaro, he told her, "We'll be in Gully Town by sundown, God willing and the creek don't rise."

"Will we stay in a white man's house?"

"Of course. Or I will. You can sleep outside on the ground if you want . . . or in a tree." He chuckled.

She vaulted up, snuggled her bottom between the dangerous horn and his soft bulge before chastising him for reminding her of the tree. "That wasn't funny. Wait until you get captured and have something like that happen to you. Then it won't be so funny."

They rode into the sun in silence, each thinking private thoughts, each sweating profusely. Occasionally Fargo shot a quick glance at the blazing ball, then around the white cloudless sky, and wondered when it would rain, or if rain was a thing of the past. The prairie grass had withered brown and dry. The soil baked till it split. It was too hot even for the flies.

At noon they crossed a dry creekbed. Sings Loud Woman had him stop. She got off the pinto and ran up the creekbed a way before she stopped and dropped onto her hands and knees. He watched her pull a square of dried, brick-hard mud back. Water appeared.

"Over here, big man," she shouted. "Water!"

He and the Ovaro came and she raised cupped hands brimful with water to him. He bent from the saddle and lapped all of the cool liquid from her hands, then licked her palms and fingers. "One more," he said, "then fill the canteen. The Ovaro gets the rest."

After giving him a second helping, she collected another cupped handful and let it dribble onto her breasts. The next went high between parted legs. Then she filled his canteen. He helped her into her riding position after the pinto had drunk the small spring-fed hole dry, then they turned their backs to the sun and continued east.

In midafternoon the air was unusually still and hot when smoke from fires in Gully Town came into view. An hour later they arrived in front of Avis' home. He heard the three women squabbling inside before Catherine noticed them and hushed the others. As he was lifting Sings Loud Woman from her hard perch, Dora appeared in the doorway.

"Well, well," she said frostily, "look what we have here. He tells us he's going out to shoot the bad guys, then comes back with an Indian whore."

Catherine pushed around her sister to get a better look at the girl. Catherine's voice trembled when she spoke to Fargo. "I don't understand, Skye. What did we do to—?"

Avis barked from behind Dora, "We didn't do anything, Catherine. That's the problem."

Fargo slapped the Ovaro's rump and sent it on its way to find water and shade. To the squint-eyed women he said, "We're thirsty as hell. I'll tell you all about it inside." He took the Indian girl by an arm and moved toward the door.

Dora stepped aside. Avis did not. "No Indian's coming

in my house," she stated matter-of-factly, and struck a defiant stance.

Fargo pushed her out of the way, tugged Sings Loud Woman inside to a water pail, and handed her the dipper.

Avis yelled, "No! She isn't putting her filthy mouth on my dipper." The miserable aunt started across the room.

Fargo's arm shot out in front of her at the chest and stopped her momentum. When Avis clawed for the dipper, the girl threw the water in her face.

Avis commenced sputtering. Fargo thought he heard a few epithets mixed in with the sounds. He pushed the angry woman back with his arm and told her, "Shut up and calm down." In Lakota he told the girl, "Go ahead and drink. They're mad at me, not you."

Avis retreated to stand at the south wall to sulk, but Dora and Catherine joined them at the pail. Avis muttered, "She isn't going with us."

Catherine agreed. So did Dora.

Fargo said, "No, Sings Loud Woman isn't going with us to California. I'm sending her back to her people."

His pronouncement completely changed the tense atmosphere in the room. All three of the pouting, sulking white women turned, showing wide smiles. They crowded around the girl and fawned over her like she was their favorite sister. Avis cooed, "Child, you must be starving half to death. We'll fry you a chicken to eat on the road, won't we, nieces?"

Fargo shook his head as he sauntered out the door, comfortable that Sings Loud Woman would be all right. He whistled the Ovaro to come to him, mounted up, then headed out of Gully Town for the ranches to the south.

Just before sundown he arrived at the Rocking 3. Several of the ranchhands saw him riding in and had the owner and his wife out on the porch of the big house when Fargo entered the front yard. He reined the horse to a halt at the front steps. Touching the brim of his hat, he said, " 'Evening, ma'am . . . sir. Name's Skye Fargo."

The balding owner came down the steps to shake the Trailsman's hand. "So, you're the big man Jud Mott told us about. Glad to meet you, Fargo. We can't repay you enough for burying our dead. My name's Otis Buckelew and this here's my wife, Sadie." Nodding to each of the ranchhands, he named them, then looked at Fargo. "Get down off that magnificent pinto." When Fargo nodded but remained in the saddle, Otis asked, "What can I do for you, Fargo? Name it. Will if I can."

Fargo cleared his throat and glanced nervously at Sadie. What he had in mind shouldn't be said in earshot of the man's wife. He answered, "Well, sir, can we, er, move over to your front gate?"

Sadie knew whatever he had to say was man talk. She smiled and said, "No, no need to do that, mister. I have a roast in the oven and need to tend to it." She turned and went inside the house.

Otis and his men collected in a knot at the bottom of the steps and looked questioningly at Fargo. He grinned and said, "I need to borrow one of your men for a few days. Young and strong would do just fine, Otis."

"That's possible." Buckelew frowned. "What for, if I may ask? Gunplay?"

"No, don't think so. I need him to take a wounded young woman north . . . to Bear Butte."

Buckelew's eyes rolled back and he whined, "Mister, you've lost all your good sense. Hellfire, man, that's wild Indian territory. You're asking me to send a man out to get scalped."

"No, sir, I'm not. He'll be safe as when he was on his ma's breast. I'd go myself if I didn't have those Bible

Boys to hunt down and kill. I've already whittled them down to three, about right for one last gunfight."

"Safe? How in the world can you promise he'd be safe up that away? Hell, man, that area is crawling with Sioux savages."

"I know that, Otis, but there's nothing to worry about in this instance. Tell him there's a wild piece of juicy red ass in it for him. She's his ticket for safety going and coming back. All he has to do is hand her over to the first Indians he sees. Simple as that. What happens between him and her on the way is up to him. However, I can promise Sings Loud Woman won't leave him alone."

"Well, I dunno," Buckelew answered feebly. "I'll put it to the boys, though. If one wants to risk losing his scalp, then that's his business. When do you want him, and where?"

"At the saloon. Tonight if he can. They need to leave at dawn."

"Yeah, well, like I said, I'll ask, but don't be surprised if nobody shows up. You're welcome to have supper with us. Sadie makes the best damn roasts this side of the Mississippi."

"Thanks, but not this time," Fargo replied. "Right now I have too much to do to stop for food. Besides, I'd gorge myself, then sleep for a month. Best I be moving on. If one wants to go, tell him the drinks are on me at the saloon. All he can hold and still be able to ride at the crack of dawn."

They watched him turn and leave through the front gate.

Fargo returned to Avis' home and found them dressed and preparing to go to bed for the night. Best of all, they acted civil for a change, even Avis. He learned she had actually asked Sings Loud Woman to sleep in bed with her. The sisters would share the smaller canopied bed. The girl wore a nightgown he figured belonged to Avis. It hid nothing. Neither did the other nightgowns. He marveled at the unusually large size of Catherine's areolae.

"The girl will be leaving at dawn," he told them. "Please see that she's up, dressed, and fed." He looked at Sings Loud Woman and repeated his instructions in her language, adding, "A young rancher is coming to take you to your people. You see to it that he isn't hurt by whoever you meet. And I want you to take care of him. Do you understand what I'm saying, what I mean?"

"Will he be big like you?" Her eyes darted to below his belt.

"Hell, girl, I don't know. Just don't hurt him. If he isn't big, make him think he is. I'll bring him to you in the morning. Sleep well."

"You aren't sleeping with that woman and me?" She looked surprised, miffed, actually. "In the tepee we—"

"No," he interrupted. "As you can see, this isn't a tepee. I'll sleep in my own bed tonight, thank you." He tipped his hat and went outside.

Catherine and Dora followed as far as the door. Dora spoke for both of them. "Big man, I don't know where you're going, but it won't be near as cozy and wild as our bed. What about it, Fargo? We'll give you a preview of what you can expect nightly on the way to California."

He chuckled as he got in the saddle. Looking at their hopeful faces, he said, "Look, no offense, ladies, but I'm not up to wrestling you two tonight. Like you said, California's a long way off. You'll get your chances . . . one at a time."

As he rode away, he heard Catherine remark to her sister, "Damn you, you said he'd do it. Now I have to wait. Damn, damn, damn."

Jud Mott and a skinny fellow Fargo had not seen before were sitting at a poker table, drinking, when he entered. Jud spoke as Fargo went behind the bar to get a bottle and a glass. "This here's Calvin Rooks, Mr. Fargo. Best piano player west of the Mississippi, he is."

Pouring from the bottle, Fargo glanced at Calvin. "You new in Gully Town?"

"No, sir. I've been working here for quite a long spell. I was out back taking a leak when all the shooting started. I took off running and didn't stop till I got winded and fell. After getting my wind back, I got up and ran some more. Been hiding out in the foothills, waiting for things to get back to normal. Got back shortly after sundown. Jud's been telling me what all you and him did, how you all ran that gang of butchers off."

Fargo looked at Mott, who obviously preferred Calvin had not made that last statement. Fargo grinned at Mott's discomfort as he tipped the glass and swigged from the whiskey. Refilling the glass, he said, "A man from the Rocking Three should arrive later. See to it that he—"

The sound of several horses pounding into Gully Town interrupted his orders to Mott. Fargo's right hand went to the Colt as his gaze settled on the swinging doors. Mott and Calvin broke and ran for the back door.

Fargo hissed, "Get your sorry asses back in here and get guns. By God, both of you are going to learn here and now how to stand and fight."

They ran upstairs and came back to cower on the top landing with rifles in their shaking hands. Fargo stepped from behind the bar ready to aim and fire. They watched six grinning men file through the swinging doors and begin slapping dust from their clothes. Fargo recognized one as being in the group when he spoke to Otis Buckelew. Fargo holstered the Colt and told Mott and Calvin, "You can see they aren't the dreaded Bible Boys, so quit shaking to pieces. You two are beginning to get on my nerves."

Turning to the cowboys, he commented, "Looks like I've got five more than I bargained for. Is anybody left at the Rocking Three?" he asked a brawny young man.

They lined up at the bar, smiling hugely, saying, "Shucks" and "Gollee." A husky young rancher drawled, "Aw, heck, Mr. Fargo, ain't but one of us goin'. You did say wild and juicy, didn't you?"

"Mott, where are your saloon keeper's manners? Get your sorry ass down here. Pour these brave men a few drinks while I sort out things. Calvin, you might as well get on that piano and entertain us while I figure out a fair way of choosing."

While they washed down mouths dry from trail dust, Fargo listened to them talk. Mostly he heard nothing other than braggadocio insofar as riding into Sioux lands was concerned, pure wishful thinking. One gave the explanation of why six came rather than one when he grumbled, "I'd fight the whole goddamn tribe for a piece now that Satisfied ain't around no more."

Another complained, "I ain't had none in a month of Sundays."

They all laughed and were still laughing when four other men strode through the doors. "Where's this guy, Skye Fargo?" one asked, and pounded the bar for a drink. "Hop to it, Mott," he barked. "We're thirsty and horny."

Calvin's bony but nimble fingers raced over the keyboard, tinkling a tune and rhythm of his own creation. Fargo centered himself behind the bar and faced the line of ten men. To the newcomers he said, "I take it you boys are from the Lazy Two Sixes, right?" They nodded and he continued, "I'm Fargo. Don't know how you heard about this, but I'll consider you just the same . . .

soon as I figure out how. In the meantime, the drinks are on the house."

"Where's Satisfied," a chubby young new arrival inquired. "I got a whopper on."

"Whack it with your gun," the man next to him suggested. "That'll close its one bad eye."

They guffawed and continued to brag and lie, getting bolder with each slug of whiskey that passed over their lower lips.

Fargo moved out from behind the bar and went to a poker table where he sat to shuffle a deck of cards. He yelled to Mott, "Saloon keeper, run those hard cases over here, then follow them with a few bottles of the cheap stuff."

There was a rush to grab seats at the table. Those not fast enough got chairs from other tables and wedged in close as possible. Mott filled glasses as Fargo explained, "High card gets the wildest ride this side of Buzzard's Gap. Playoff to break a tie. Everyone agreed?" The only sound in the saloon came from the piano. "Mott, go tell your friend to take a break."

When the piano fell silent, Fargo asked if anyone wanted to cut the deck. Ten pairs of hands shot out on top of the table. He set the deck in the center of the table and let each man cut once, restacking the deck after each cut had been made. Leaving the cards out in the center, Fargo slipped the one on top off and slid it facedown to the man on his left, then did the same for the others until all ten men had a card. Glancing among their perspiring faces, he asked, "Okay, fellows, somebody has to turn over first. Or do I count to three and have all flip at the same time?"

"No," someone muttered. "One at a time."

"Agreed?" Fargo asked.

"Yeah," another seconded. "But who goes first?"

Fargo sighed disgustedly. He felt like changing his mind and simply picking one of them, but he'd gone this far and he couldn't stop now to change the rules. He spun an empty whiskey bottle dead-center on the table. Twenty-six nervous eyes watched the bottle spin until it stopped, the neck pointing at a lanky kid. The young man gulped, turned over the nine of clubs, and said, "Aw, shit."

Nine men sighed. Fargo twirled the bottle again.

The neck aimed at a tall robust young man, who smiled hopefully as he flipped over his card, then tore it in half when he and everyone else saw the two of diamonds. The lanky kid holding the nine spots exhaled mightily and slumped in his chair. The loser mumbled, "Well, it's back to Miss Tillie Five Fingers for me."

In spinning succession the bottle's neck turned over the eight of spades, ten of clubs, five of hearts, then the ace of hearts. The bearded owner of it, a strong young cowhand, let out a war whoop that rattled the rafters. "Tell me it will take a month to get wherever it is I'm going," he chortled.

"Piss on you, Rafferty," one of the men still in contention snorted. "There's three more of 'em in there and I got one." In a more subdued voice he added, "I just gotta have an ace."

The randomly rotating bottle gave him the chance to prove it. When the big fellow took a deep breath and held it, Rafferty goaded him. "Ain't so damn sure, are you, Smiley, when the time for truth arrives? Go ahead. Show us whatcha got."

Smiley's jaws ballooned from the big breath he held as he eased the card over with his eyes shut. He snapped them open when he heard one of the others say, "Well, I'll be damned." When Smiley saw he'd caught the ace of diamonds, he sank back in his chair, exhaling loudly.

Dawson caught the jack of spades and George Peabody ripped his three of hearts to shreds and threw the pieces into the air. As they fell like confetti, Fargo looked at the sole remaining challenger, a deeply tanned young man with an angelic face he estimated about age twenty, who was really sweating.

"C'mon, Sweet Cyrus, quit stalling and get it over with," Smiley coaxed from his slouched position in the chair. "Waiting won't change the damn spots."

Fargo watched Cyrus' left trembling hand as it reached for the card. Cyrus also closed his eyes before he turned it over. Rafferty's gasp snapped Cyrus' eyes open. Along with everyone else, Cyrus saw the ace of spades. The young man stood, smiled broadly, sat, got back to his feet, then sat again before suggesting, "What say all three of us take her north? I'll share. I don't mind none."

"No," Fargo replied testily. "I said any tie gets to draw again." He collected the cards and shuffled up. As he did, he explained, "No bottle this time, men. You turn them over at the same time, on my count of three." He offered the deck to each man for cutting. All refused. Fargo fanned the deck in an arc across the table and told them, "Choose your own poison, gentlemen."

Smiley drew a card from near the center of the spread, Rafferty picked the second from one end, and Cyrus took the card that would have been on top if the deck were upright. Fargo slow-counted to three. They flipped over their cards. Rafferty held the five of hearts, Smiley the four of spades. Cyrus nearly fainted when he saw his ace of clubs.

"Lucky bastard," someone growled. The losers returned to the bar to drink and think about what might have been.

Calvin picked up where he left off on the music. Fargo eyed Cyrus, who asked, "What happens now?"

"You'll meet Sings Loud Woman in the morning," Fargo told him.

Cyrus scrambled to his feet, his smile about to bust his lips. He looked at Fargo and pled, "Morning? I can't wait that long, Mr. Fargo. Please, sir, let me have her now. I'm too wide awake to sleep—regular, that is. Hell, I'm ready to ride. Long trip, you know. Please?"

Fargo gave it a moment's thought and reckoned, Why not? Like the kid said, there was no way he'd get any sleep for thinking about it. He said, "Fine with me, cowboy. Don't see no reason for you to hang around here." He looked at Mott, told him to go wake up Avis. "Tell her to get the Indian girl dressed. Then you bring her to the saloon. No side trips to the haystack, Mott. Got that?"

Mott nodded throughout the big man's instructions.

The young cowboy sat, stared at the wall, and said, "Gollee, I can't believe this is really happening to me." He broke the stare and looked up at Fargo. "Don't say nothing to the others, but this is going to be my first time. I get all dizzy and wobble-kneed just thinking about it."

The big man grinned, patted him on the shoulder. "Well, pardner, this time tomorrow night you'll be a veteran of at least one scrap with an Indian. She's sure as hell going to take something from you, but it won't be your scalp. Foreskin, maybe," he added.

Fargo went to the bar. Wedging in between two of the men, he poured himself a whiskey. "Sweet Cyrus is leaving shortly," he announced, knowing what would follow.

Rafferty turned and looked at Cyrus' backside a split second before pushing away from the bar and going to him. When he did, the others glanced over their shoulders at him. Fargo watched their eyes dart left and right momentarily, then they rushed to beat Rafferty to the man.

On the way they all spoke at once. "Hey, Cyrus, I'll give you ten dollars to take your place," offered one. "I'll up that to fifteen," another quoted quickly. "Piker! I'll go twenty-five," a chubby cowboy said. And so it went until the amount was up to a staggering two hundred before they all crowded around the table.

Cyrus was tempted and on the verge of giving in when Mott came through the doors with Sings Loud Woman. The bidding trickled off, then ceased altogether as first one then another of the men saw her standing just inside the room. Mott cleared his throat and croaked, "Here she is, Mr. Fargo. Want you to know them other women said this ain't right. That's why she's still in her nightdress. I think they're expecting you to send her back, especially that Avis."

Cyrus gulped.

Fargo ordered, "Get up out of that chair and come with me."

Everyone followed Fargo and Cyrus to Sings Loud Woman. When she looked into Fargo's eyes, he spoke to her in Lakota. "Don't be afraid. They're not all going." He put a hand on the cowboy's shoulder and continued. "This is Cyrus. He's a good man. Look after him and don't hurt him too bad. He will probably cry and holler for his mama, but don't worry about that. He wants to head out now. That all right with you?"

She shrugged. All the men gulped when they saw her bosom jiggle during the movement. She asked, "Is he big as you, Bull Buffalo-Prick Man?"

"Hell, I don't know," he answered. "Like I've already

told you, I didn't strip them and look. For all I know he's bigger."

"Will I see you again?"

"No." He nodded for her to go outside, then turned to the winner. "Cyrus, get your horse ready." The big man shifted to Jud behind the bar. "Mott, give him a bottle or two, plus something for them to eat on the way."

Rafferty mumbled, "Eat? Looks to me like he's got enough to choke on already. Dammit to hell, I started to take that top card. My own damn fault. Now I'll never know what's between those long legs."

Cyrus packed the bottles and grub in his saddlebags as Jud handed them to him. Then Cyrus turned and asked Fargo, "Uh, er, sir, where's her horse?"

Fargo patted the front part of the saddle. "Right here, cowpuncher, right where she can make that horn go limp." He smiled.

Rafferty came over and said, "Tell you what, Cyrus, I'll give you three hundred and this here belt buckle my daddy gave me just before he died." He raised the bottom of the huge silver buckle so Cyrus could see the state of Texas done in relief and the several pieces of dull red glass mounted on it.

Cyrus took a deep breath, put a foot in the stirrup, slipped, and fell clumsily to the ground.

Fargo picked him up and tossed him up onto the saddle. "Boy, I keep telling you to quit doing that. Next time I won't be around. Now, scoot back and make room for her little ass."

Cyrus was quick to obey. Fargo gripped Sings Loud Woman at the waist, lifted her up, gave her a good-bye kiss that brought a chorus of "Awww's" from the men, then hoisted her into position on the saddle.

All the men groaned as they watched her squirm her

buttocks and snuggle back against Cyrus, whose eyes crossed and shoulders sagged. Only Fargo, Cyrus, and the Indian girl knew for certain that she had worked her cheeks apart to accommodate the cowboy's bulge. She glanced at Fargo, shook her head slightly, and in Lakota commented, "His name is Puppy Dog-Prick Man."

Fargo slapped the horse's flanks to send them on their way. Everyone stood in the street, hoping Cyrus would faint and fall to the ground. All they saw was the horse's rump as it vanished into the night north of Gully Town.

6

Fargo drank with the losers until he glanced toward the entrance and saw Dora, Catherine, and Avis peering inside. He went to the doors and said, "Go home. This isn't a proper place for proper ladies. Now, scat, all three of you."

"Fargo, you're the meanest son of a bitch I ever met," Dora snarled. "Those fellers are dying to get satisfied. You know they are. Poor things. Won't take me but a few minutes. How about it . . . for old time's sake?"

"No. Dammit, I said go home."

Catherine stuck her tongue out at him, then spun and walked away. Avis quickly followed her, but Dora tried again to get inside. "C'mon, big man, let me in. They need me."

He shook his head. When she pressed against the doors, he stared her to a halt and warned, "Set one foot in here and so help me I'll spank you until it's too raw to do anything."

"You wouldn't."

"You'd be too sore to ride. Go home, Dora, and sleep it off."

"Will I see you tomorrow?"

"Of course. We head west after breakfast."

"Can I satisfy you on the way?"

"Don't know why not."

She nodded, sighed at the immediate loss, then shot him a wink and walked away, shouting for the other two to wait up.

Fargo watched her bouncing fanny until she disappeared in the darkness. He fetched a lamp and went upstairs to Dora's room to sleep. While undressing at one of the windows in the darkened room, he looked out, hoping to see potential rain clouds, but saw the full moon in a star-studded sky. The big man scratched his back and muscled behind as he went to sprawl on Dora's sweet-smelling bed. Shoving the Colt under the pillow, he closed his eyes. Sleep came swiftly.

When Fargo's wild-creature hearing detected a barely audible sound out on the balcony, he opened one eye and eased his big Colt from under the pillow. A soft, slow melody played by Calvin filtered up the stairs, was muted further by the long hallway and the room's closed and locked door.

The still, hot night that enveloped Gully Town absorbed whatever amount of Calvin's music that escaped through the shattered saloon windows and open front doors. The moon had moved into the sky's northwest quadrant, denying the room direct moonlight. Fargo stared toward the door and listened for the sound that had awakened him.

Slowly, naturally for a sleeping man, he rolled his powerfully built body onto its right side and peered through the totally dark room at the open twin windows. He hoped the scant light spilling out of the saloon below and into the street might be enough to show him the nocturnal intruder's silhouette.

Should have pulled those flimsy curtains back, or jerked them down, he thought. He strained to see through them.

The same soft sound came again. Barefoot, he muttered to himself. As he cocked the Colt's hammer and held it ready to swing and fire, he drew the sheet over it and up to his muscled waist.

Part of a dark form appeared at the sill of the window to his left. Fargo fired. The form quickly poked up above the other sill. He fired again, only to see it reappear at the first sill. A frown formed on his face when he heard the night visitor giggle and saw the small silhouette, which he recognized now as the crown of a hat, start moving back and forth along the sill.

Now he grinned, although his visitor was playing a most dangerous game. Sure of himself, he said, "I'm tired of playing shooting gallery. If you want to talk, come on in. If you want to die, stay there and fool with me."

He watched the silhouette of a boy rise from safety below the sill and put the hat on. A pair of boots were tossed inside the room, then the boy crawled through the open window and stood enveloped by the billowy curtains.

"Pull that trigger again and you're a daid man," a clear, husky female voice warned. "I ain't here to kill you," her drawl added quickly. "That'll happen later. You are Skye Fargo, ain't you, the one they call the Trailsman?"

"One and same," Fargo replied easily. He let her hear the hammer be uncocked. "Who the hell are you?" he asked in a friendly tone. "And what are you up to, sneaking around on my balcony in the middle of the night? You asking to get killed?" He struck a match and moved the flame above the lamp's wick, then paused when he saw the muzzle of a Smith & Wesson peek between the curtains, aimed straight above the bridge of his nose. Not at all amused, he growled, "Honey, you better holster that damn gun before I get mad and hurt you." Sweetie, he thought, you got one coming for playing silly games with me.

Just as the match burned his fingers and went out, he watched the muzzle lower, then retreat. Fargo struck another match. During the flaring he watched the curtains part. A lovely, petite woman took one pace forward before holstering her weapon. Their eyes met as she unbuckled the large gun belt that rode low on her marvelous hips. He watched her full lips form into an impish grin. The heavy belt fell to the wood floor.

Fargo touched the flame to the wick, then propped himself up on one elbow.

Holding the grin and eye contact, she began unbuttoning her loose-fitting checked shirt. Fargo became aroused instantly by the provocative unveiling. She bared one breast for a teasing second, then covered it quickly and waited for his reaction. He accommodated her by wetting his lips. She drew the fronts of the shirt back and let it fall to the floor, exposing both firm breasts that, like the rest of her upper body, glistened from a film of perspiration. Then, as he continued to watch, she moistened both thumbs and forefingers and pulled on her proud pink nipples.

"I like this game a whole lot better," Fargo said through a smile.

She came halfway to the bed, stopped, and slowly began unbuttoning her fly. After a long pause designed to pique his curiosity even more, she hooked her thumbs in the Levi's waistband and her bloomers. She drew both down until only the top part of her bushy black, curly pubic hair glistened in the lamplight. Fargo's smile widened. She raised her right hand to a breast, cupped and squeezed it, then traced her fingers down over her indented belly button, paused when the middle finger touched hair, then slipped the finger down and out of his sight and began massaging with it.

Fargo added the second elbow for a prop. "Okay, honey, you've got me warmed up. You coming to bed, or do you have something else exciting to show?"

She closed the distance to the bed by half before stopping to wiggle out of the Levi's.

"Wiggle some more," Skye suggested, for her bouncing breasts were the best part of her teasings so far.

She flipped the Levi's and bloomers next to the bed with her toes, turned her unblemished firm round buttocks to him, parted her feet by about a yard, and watched his eyes. Tensing her rump muscles, a dimple appeared on each cheek. Then she relaxed them and brought her feet together.

After another sweaty pause, she bent and touched her toes with one hand, tantalizing Fargo with the magnificent display of bushy black the sensual pose produced. Holding the pose, she spread her feet apart again. The ebony parted, and so did the tight glistening crack that materialized when it did.

Her head lowered and she looked between her breasts and thighs at him. As he stared at her youthful inlet, her hand came up and teased the curly sable surrounding it. He watched her middle finger come to the slit and ease the lips apart, then her forefinger gesture for him to come and get it.

When she saw the sheet at his crotch begin to rise, she broke the sultry pose and spun around with her coalblack eyes riveted on the rising. The lovely childlike woman pursed her full lips, bowed her eyebrows in pleasurable awe.

Fargo watched her eyes increasingly widen and the corners of her lips turn up to form a devilish grin. When the sheet reached full peak, obviously towering beyond her expectations, she looked at his handsome chiseled face. Her breathing quickened as she ran her pink tongue over her lips, clearly implying she wanted, intended to taste him.

A tiny gurgle escaped through her lips as she came to stand by the bed. She looked down into his lake-blue eyes, as though just seeing them for the first time. She bent at the waist, worked her shoulders forward and back so the breasts would swing invitingly over his mouth.

His gaze focused first on her pink nipples, then on the half-dollar-sized creamy-pink areolae encircling them. He believed the smooth breasts had not yet seen their twenty-first birthday. Fargo's heartbeat increased with anticipation as the tip of his tongue involuntarily moistened his lips.

She bent farther and dragged the right nipple over his lips, whispering, "Think you can handle me? Don't be fooled by my tiny size." Before he could answer, she urged the nipple between his waiting lips.

Fargo eagerly took the erect nipple, areolae, and as much of the breast as his mouth could hold, and sucked. As he relished her savory taste, he wrapped a muscled arm around her slim waist, pulled her closer, and let his fingers explore the source of the wetness he found around the black curly hair.

A rapturous low moan came through her parted lips as she maneuvered her opening so the probing finger would glide up and down over it. "Wait," she gasped. "I forgot to take off my damn hat."

Fargo heard the hat skip across the floor to a window. He shifted to the other nipple as he felt her long raven hair, now loose and flowing, caress his face. She raised up, withdrawing the nipple and breast from his mouth, then entered the bed to kneel beside him. Through a wide smile, she whispered, "Big man, there ain't no way it's gonna go in me unless it's good an' slippery first."

Fargo's right hand stayed on her head as she kissed her

way down his powerful chest, over his muscled torso, then take in and wet as much of his immensity as her mouth and lips would conform around and her craving tongue could slicken.

She came off it, making a sucking sound, and murmured, "Jesus, was that ever delicious . . . so damn good . . . best I ever had."

He pulled her warm body atop his own and felt her flat belly heaving, almost spasmodic, hungry for him to enter her. But he took a breast instead and sucked on it ravenously and made no move to accommodate her. After a torrid moment of breathless bliss, she pulled his face from the breast and kissed him openmouthed. Her hot tongue explored as though a long drought was over, as though it might return in the next second. Her warmth squirmed and mashed against his muscled body as she writhed constantly.

The Trailsman's mind swirled in ecstasy when he felt her soft hand grasp his length and squeeze firmly. "Damn, mister, you *are* big," she murmured between hot gasps. "Mebbe I won't kill you, after all."

Straddling him, she raised her hips and worked his hot blood-swollen crown into her moisture-laden sheath. "Oh, God, oh, God, yes," she moaned, and bore down with all her might to capture him fully.

"Jesus," she squealed. "Oh, God, you're in places that . . . Aaeeiiii! In places no man has reached," she grunted. He felt her thrust downward and arch her back to drive him deeper. Through gritted teeth she groaned, "Damn, you're big around."

Fargo rolled her under his muscular body. Her slim legs locked high around his waist. Grunting and groaning, both gyrated their hips slowly and in harmony, then moved them faster and faster, wildly. "Oh, my God," she whimpered when half his powerful shaft was lost.

"Deeper, Fargo, deeper! All of it! Please, give me all of it!"

He stabbed downward and romped upward as hard as he could, then grabbed her tense buttocks and welded her to him even tighter. "Oh, yes, yes, yes," she cried unabashedly. "Oh, God, that's so good, so hot . . . so filling."

Fargo felt her shapely ass rise as her legs unlocked, then her ankles came up and hooked around his strong neck. She was pumping furiously now, frantically, as if suddenly seized by an overpowering urge to have the gargantuan erection rip her asunder. Her voice became louder as she whimpered ceaselessly, begging him to make it last forever. "More," she gasped. "Oh, God please don't stop. More . . . oh, please don't stop. Faster, Fargo, faster, deeper. Oh, God, yes, yes, oh, yes . . . that's it," she screamed.

He felt her many contractions that came in prelude to the massive one that clamped hard around his throbbing shaft. "Aaeeiiii," she cried with delighted anticipation when her viselike contraction began squeezing, milking, and she repeated the heavenly cry until he flooded her.

When Fargo slackened the pounding, she screamed, "More, damn you, more! Don't quit . . . oh, please, don't quit!"

Exhausted, Fargo lay there with the little woman's legs refusing to release him while she continued to struggle on his limpness, trying hard to bring it back, cursing him for not making it last longer. "Lady, it's over," he said. "Let go of me for now."

"No it ain't," she complained, and urged her soggy sheath upward. "It ain't over till I say so, and I ain't said."

Fargo forced her legs apart and rolled off her. "Hellfire, ma'am, a man's got to have some rest between satisfying hot fillies like you. Where'd you come from, anyhow? How'd you know to look for me here? Who told you my name? Who in the hell are you, anyhow?"

Her expression showed she was miffed. She didn't answer right away. Fargo watched her leave the bed and step to the porcelain washbowl atop the small table. Pouring water from the matching wide-mouth jar, she snapped, "Jezebel."

Fargo rolled the name around in his mind and searched for a clue while watching her clean her thighs and crotch with a dampened towel. Not finding one, he said, "Name means nothing to me. Should it?"

"It will," she said, and tossed the towel onto his stomach. Stepping back to stand at the bed, she said calmly, "You're better, a whole lot bigger down there than my brothers."

Fargo looked at her anew. When she cocked her head and pursed her lips, Fargo winked and said, "Now, honey, I reckon I got my strength back. Hop back on the bed. Get up on your knees. You might grab hold of the headboard, too, 'cause I'm going to try my damnedest to pound through you and shove your pretty head plumb through that wall."

Jezebel flashed him a wide wicked smile and quickly assumed the position. Looking over her shoulder, she suggested, "Shove hard and deep, big man. That'll be my sweet ass shoving back." She laid her head on the pillow, reached back, and spread her cheeks for him.

Fargo shoved and pounded. She shrieked, gasped, and screamed. For every devastating thrust he made, she retaliated by levering against the headboard to swallow him full. He lifted her by the waist until her knees left the bed, then doubled her over as he rammed into her deepest, hottest recesses. She hollered and grunted, reached under his long strokes, and grabbed his swinging balls and squeezed, screaming, "Explode, damn you! Aaeeiiii . . . more, more, more . . . harder . . . rougher!"

He couldn't believe what he was hearing. He thrust harder, lifted her ass high, and gave her all he had.

"Aaeeiiii," she shrieked. When he withdrew most of his length, her legs curled around his thighs in her struggle for complete release from the last inch of his manliness still inside the wet slit. She screamed louder than ever when he hammered into her pistonlike and nearly flattened her to the headboard.

"Oh, oh, oh," she cried. "You're killing me . . . tearing me wide open. Oh, goddamn, that hurts so good."

"That's just the ante," he grunted, and kept his murderous pace.

When his volcano blew, she shrieked she'd had enough. "You're settin' me on fire in there! Lemme go, I've had all of you I can take. Goddamn, that burns."

He released her, collapsed backward onto the bed, and lay panting while listening to her whimper. Slowly she rose, left the bed to get and drag the wet towel through her dark V. After wiping her thighs, she wadded the towel and threw it at him. He watched her retrieve her clothes, then pull them on and don her hat. She strapped on the gun belt while standing at a window.

Putting a foot over the sill, she bent to step out on the balcony. Pausing, she snarled, "You shot and killed my brothers, Luke and Matthew."

Fargo's eyes widened. He'd thought the Hanks were all men. Now it looked like he was wrong. She was the short one he saw riding the big dun into the saloon, who freely admitted she engaged in incest. "Your pa and other brother are next." His hand groped under the pillows to find the Colt, but she'd obviously found and moved it while he pounded her into submission.

She stepped out onto the balcony, looked back at him

through the curtains, and dropped the Colt. "Uh, huh. You'll have to get past me first, Skye Fargo, and it ain't so easy to get by Jezebel Hanks. Tonight all I did was satisfy a curiosity, have a little pleasure while sizing you up. Next time we meet, I'm gonna pull the trigger and blow your goddamn head off. Needn't rush over and get your gun to shoot me. It's unloaded, big man." She pitched the bullets over the balcony railing.

He believed she'd damn sure try to kill him when they next met. "I'll be waiting," he said, "but I don't shoot females. Neither do I let them shoot me. That's a riddle for you to figure out."

She snorted sarcastically, then stepped out of his sight.

Fargo came off the bed, grabbed his gun belt, and was removing bullets from it as he went through the window. Picking up the empty Colt, he scanned the street below to maybe see her riding off. But he neither saw nor heard the dun pounding out of town. Reloading at the balcony railing, he reckoned she was faster than he imagined. Jezebel Hanks was gone.

But the Trailsman would find her. He would find all three when daylight showed him the way. Then he'd put a fast end to their butchering ways.

7

Fargo arose before first light, took his clothes downstairs, and dressed while sipping whiskey from a bottle. Three lamps still burned in the messy room. Empty bottles and glasses were strewn everywhere, and the unmistakable odor of alcohol permeated the room, testifying the drunken losers had made a night of it.

He knew they were in no condition to ride and must be sleeping in the rooms upstairs. He wanted to ask Mott a few questions before heading out. Fargo took the bottle and a lamp with him when he went up to find the man. Nudging a door open with his foot, he poked the lamp inside.

At first glance he wondered why five stark-naked cowboys would sleep together on one bed when there was plenty of comfortable flooring to spread out on. Shaking his head, he drew the lamp back, blinked, and stuck it back inside. Now he saw the reason. One ass among the heap belonged to Satisfied. She'd sneaked back to the saloon for one final fling.

Well, he thought, somebody sure as hell got satisfied. He left the door open when he stepped away and went to the next.

Nudging it open, he held the lamp in front of him and

counted not one or four but six bare asses in the bed. "Shit," he mumbled, and shook his head. He recognized what he presumed was Catherine's rump poking up out of the pack. They were all snoring softly, about as far from reality as any could get.

He went inside the next room and stood looking down on the pianist, saloon keeper . . . and Avis. The two men lay bellydown with spittle leaking from their open mouths. Aunt Avis was on her back with both hands buried under their bodies at the groin. Her face indicated she'd gone to sleep mad as hell about something. To his surprise he saw she had a fantastic bush of dark-brown pubic hair. Her breasts were about the size of a champagne glass. The nipples were large as a thimble and the brownish-pink areolae skimpy but nice. Although all three women had defied his orders, he'd actually expected it, so he wasn't upset to find them here.

Fargo tapped Mott's butt with the bottle. The kid nearly jumped out of his skin when he glanced over his shoulder and saw Fargo staring down at him. The Trailsman nodded toward the door, then went out and down to the saloon.

Mott came hurrying behind him, dancing a jig on the stairs as he worked first one leg in his britches, then the other. "Yes, sir, Mr. Fargo, what can I do for you this morning?" He glanced outside and muttered, "It is morning, ain't it?"

"Better be or I'm not yet up. What the hell happened here last night after I went to bed? I thought I told you Dora wasn't to set foot in this place again."

Mott's discomfort showed in several places, especially in his eyes, which wouldn't stay on Fargo's. "Well, sir, I got outvoted, pure and simple. Rafferty, he said he'd bounce me off all the walls and ceiling if I didn't let her in. I believed him 'cause he was holding me kinda high up by my shirt collar.

"Anyhow, Smiley and Rafferty, they went and got 'em. Things got wild as hell in here, what with three women. Dora, she pulled off her nightdress first thing, then Rafferty, he picked her up and stood her on the bar. Calvin played the music while she danced and strutted. Hell, Mr. Fargo, everbody got drunk as a Virginia skunk.

"Me and Calvin, we ended up in bed with Avis. We were drunk. I guess I ain't much of a saloon keeper, either. Do I have to give it back to you?"

Fargo could understand. Hell, it was no contest. Nine to one—twelve if you counted in three horny females—was no match for the little guy. He'd censure the women later. "I had a visitor last night. That's what I want to talk to you about."

"Visitor?" Mott's stunned expression was genuine.

"Yes. A tiny female with a gorgeous behind."

Mott smiled and relaxed. "Oh, you mean her. She—"

"You saw her?"

"Sure thing, Mr. Fargo. We all did. She wandered in through the back door 'bout an hour before Rafferty and Smiley went to get the aunt and sisters. Tiny little thing, pretty as a picture and raring to go, if you know what I mean." Mott bounced his eyebrows.

"And?"

"She climbed up on the bar, grabbed a drink from one of the men, and drank it down like a man who needed a drink real bad. Then she looked us over and started shucking her clothes. Damnedest sight any of us ever saw. Lots better'n Dora's show. Before it was over she had three of them cowhands buck-naked and put on a show for us with them one at a time. I mean, this here bar and that poker table over yonder and Calvin's piano ain't never gonna be the same no more.

"That little whore, she's got more moves than castor oil can put on you. Yessiree-Bob. Uh, huh. All we could do was stand there and watch, stare. After it was all over and she left, Frank Richardson, he was one of the three she picked out, he told us she wasn't so good. Said she was real loose. Said it was like sticking it in a can of lard. Said she must've just got it off a fence post."

Fargo could believe that. "Mott, that was Jezebel Hanks."

Jud flinched and simply stared at the big man for a moment while the full impact of what he'd just heard registered in his addled brain. Finally he gasped, "You sure 'bout that? You ain't kidding me, are you, Mr. Fargo? Trying to scare me for letting Satisfied back in?"

"It was her, all right. Came in through a balcony window with a gun in her hand. Left the same way. Before she did, she told me her name and said I'd killed her brothers, Matthew and Luke. Which way did she go?"

"Went back out the same way she came in. I heard her ride off and stepped outside to get another look at that sweet behind of hers. She rode north, fast as hell." Mott paused and shifted his weight to the other foot before adding, "She knows about that Indian girl. Smiley mentioned Cyrus winning and taking her north. That seemed to make her mad for a minute or two. And there's another thing you ought to know. While she was pulling on her clothes, she said she'd be back and take on the ones she missed."

"Okay. That's what I wanted to know. You can go back to bed now. When the women wake up and after they can't take any more of being wallowed on, tell them what I just told you and that I've gone after the Bible Boys." Fargo moved for the door.

Mott followed him as far as the porch and asked, "Got any idea when you might be back? Got any new orders for me?"

Fargo kept walking as he said, "No to both questions. But I advise all of you to keep your guns loaded and cocked. They're in the neighborhood. They could, and probably will, return when you least expect."

Mott looked furtively up and down the street before he went in the saloon to have a drink or two to calm his trembling body.

Fargo proceeded to the livery and got the Ovaro ready to ride. He walked the pinto to the end of the street, then went to a faster gait, heading north in pursuit of Jezebel. He felt sure that she would lead him to her brother and Noah, and that he'd see the dun's tracks soon.

He followed the route he believed any person stupid enough to go north would take if they were in a big hurry—the path of least resistance. He avoided the sharper rises on the rolling landscape and stayed in the lower, flatter places. When it was light enough for him to see clearly, he spotted hoofprints and noted she had the dun in a canter.

The farther he rode, the more he wished her trail would swing to the right. She was following along the eastern edge of the Black Hills, and that was dangerous, although they were still well to the west.

At noon he came down a long sloping hill that merged with another, more pronounced, at the bottom. Her trail went up the new hill rather than around it. At the top of it he discovered why. Not only did he find the cold remains of a small fire, he also saw the hoofprints of two other shod horses. He dismounted to rest the stallion, then walked a circle. He found where they left. Their trail continued north.

"Damn," he mumbled. "This isn't good. They're heading straight into the Sioux on their way to Bear Butte for the great council."

As Fargo walked back to the Ovaro, it occurred to him that he hadn't seen any signs left by Cyrus and Sings Loud Woman. That told him she knew a shorter route and put Cyrus on it. And that meant they were crossing through most of He Sapa.

He shook his head as he returned to the saddle. He estimated the trio of reckless killers were about six hours ahead of him, and he noticed they weren't in a big hurry to get wherever the hell they were going. He rode down the far side of the hill and through a shallow creek at its base. Both he and the horse paused to drink. He filled his canteen, then splashed water on his face and doused his hair.

Within the hour he passed a butte off to his right, then came down onto a meadow much later. As Fargo was riding through tall grass, a fat porcupine scurried for cover when the horse barely missed the animal. A few minutes later he came to another narrow creek and dismounted. Fargo considered the Hanks' trail and concluded they had absolutely no idea as to what lay ahead, and he didn't mean the Sioux.

If they continue to go north, he thought, they will tread where damn few Indians go. Returning to the saddle, he shook his head.

He stopped at sundown and stared at the most barren and desolate of all the arid lands he'd ever seen—the uninhabited Badlands. It was an expansive island of nothingness surrounded by the great plains on three sides and the Black Hills on the other. Here not one blade of grass, not even one tough cactus, or one drop of water could be found . . . only a myriad of gulches dry as a sunbaked bone. Even the remarkably resilient buffalo skirted this land and no buzzard wasted its effort to scavenge, for there was nothing for it to find.

The Badlands were a true torture chamber in the sun. Throughout the summer months the fiery earth and unmoving air were hotter than the hinges on the gates to hell. Fargo knew neither he nor the pinto could make it across during the day, and he wondered if they could at night, but he had to try. God, but it made him thirsty to just think about the long passage.

Night fell like a million thunders and left him in near-total darkness. As it did, the lack of cloud cover allowed the heat to rise swiftly from the surface. The temperature dropped dramatically and he rode in comfortable, cooler air.

No longer able to see the murderers' trail, he rode blindly, weaving the pinto through the endless gulches onto the longer flat stretches whenever possible. Away to his left the ragged crest of weather-carved tall hills rose from the otherwise flat terrain. His Sioux friends from the Two Kettles and Brule bands had told him this place was taboo, that many Nagis lived here and that they didn't want to be bothered. They whispered when telling the story to him, as though their spirits had long-range hearing and might strike them dead for making the revelation to a white man, friend or no.

Fargo dwelt on this remembrance as he wound his way ever northward. As he thought, a phenomena of great magnitude and personal awe occurred. He instantly became alarmed when the ice-cold wind tore at his buckskin coat. Holding his hat down in the shrieking wind, he saw the stars collect in a majestic, sparkling ball that illuminated the terrain clear as day. As he watched, they exploded outward from the ball's center and rained down.

At the end of their fall all burned out. He was left in a black void, unable to tell one direction from another. With the blackness came mournful voices carried in the wind. He listened intently to the babble and discerned a voice he thought he'd heard before. Yes, he remembered, it's the old Miniconju man crying out to me.

"I hear you, Grandfather," Fargo shouted into the wind.

The wind cried, "Go back, go back. You have crossed the line."

Then, as abruptly as it had manifested, the phenomena ended and with it went the coldness and wind. Fargo glanced to the sky and saw both moon and stars. He trudged onward.

Sometime after midnight the moon reached its zenith, and from its bright glow he saw his quarry's tracks. They too were trying to find their way out of the labyrinth while keeping an eye on the jagged outline of the crest to his left.

At sunrise he punched out of the last gulch and the Badlands onto grassy terrain. Still no signs of water, though. He watched the ground more closely now, for the tall prairie grass often hid the threesome's tracks. They were definitely intent on proceeding north, though he could not imagine a destination, for there was nothing ahead but more of the same. They were well into Sioux territory, where damn few white men had ever been and where none was allowed to build a town of any size. A handful of Frenchmen had set up trading posts, but they were few and far between, definitely isolated.

In this region supplies were unheard of. Like Elmer Dugan, most of the trapper-traders were squaw men, content to live in complete freedom and to hell with worldly materialism. Game was plentiful, and so was nightly love. Fargo couldn't fault the life, although he preferred his own particular brand of freedom.

Miles later, he came over a long rise and saw a river coursing southeast in the floor of a wooded valley. On its bank he saw where the Bible Boys had stopped. He got off his horse and let him drink. Fargo shucked his clothes, jumped in, and tried to drink the river dry. After relishing the wet respite, he arranged his clothes and gun belt under the saddlebags and on the saddle for crossing to the far side of the river. Moments later he was following the Bible Boys' tracks again.

They led him upstream and he had to chuckle at their obvious misery. Having finally found water, they were clearly staying next to it. Fargo had no idea where the stream led, and he felt positive they didn't, either.

At sunset the river presented him with an ominous panorama of He Sapa from its eastern side. The hills, dotted with lush green foliage and towering ponderosa, stood black as sin itself, tempting and discouraging at the same time. He knew he was close behind his quarry, but he might lose them in the dark. He suspected the Bible Boys were in lands foreign to them and had no idea where they were going. In the dark, they too would stop, wait for the moon to rise and show the way, maybe even sleep until morning's first light.

Fargo dismounted and spread his bedroll on the ground, then lay down to sleep.

Shortly before daybreak his wild-creature hearing snapped his eyes open. He lay still, listening. Off to his left a dry twig cracked, the barely audible sound pulling his gaze toward it. His right hand eased from the bedroll with his unholstered Colt ready. He waited and watched. Six white-tail deer stepped from the dense scrub less than ten feet away and moved to the bank for water. The buck, he noticed, came last, and in the dim light Fargo counted eight points on its antlers. He relaxed and waited for the deer to finish before he sat up. All six vanished in the blink of an eye.

He washed up, then mounted and nibbled on jerky while he followed the Bible Boys' trail again. By mid-morning the sun beat down on him with renewed fury. By noon the heat was almost unbearable, and by midafternoon he felt baked and relieved to see the beginning of the island forest.

"I don't care how sacred it is," he muttered to the Ovaro, "we're going in."

Fargo quickly discovered that this green canopy, unlike the many others, trapped most all moisture, and the crisp smell of pine hung heavy in the sultry air. He began sweating profusely the moment he rode beneath the branches.

The forest and hills were alive with creatures large and small. He watched and listened to them as he followed alongside the stream into a dark canyon. A pair of eagles left their aerie, gained altitude, then soared gracefully out of the canyon. Millions of little white butterflies flitted down the canyon as far as he could see, and the staccato of a woodpecker, after a tree worm, echoed off the sheer rocky walls. In short order he saw both raccoons and black bears fishing in reeds where the stream widened and created a calm cove. He watched one of the small bears pluck a trout from the water and juggle the slippery meal onto dry land. He felt at home again.

The stream led him out of the dark canyon into one that was even more serene and beautiful, then meandered between pine and birch-infested hills. Rounding yet another bend, he broke through a stand of red willows and halted abruptly.

On the hillside to his right stood many scaffolds. There

was no question about it in his mind now: he was in Sioux burial grounds, the very place he'd been warned not to go. But there on the ground where the Ovaro stood were three sets of shod hoofprints. They too had stopped to look and wonder, then kept going upstream as he did.

Moments later he came to other scaffolds on the hillsides on both sides of the narrow stream. He pressed on, eyeing the burial ground and shod hoofprints.

Fargo came to a small meadow as the blazing sun lowered behind the hills on his left. Darkness seemed to fall at lightning speed, and once again the coolness settled in. He dismounted and rested with his back against a huge oak on the fringe of the meadow, waiting for the moon to appear and show him the way.

Hours later he went to the grazing Ovaro, climbed in the saddle, and quickly picked up their trail. After doggedly following it until after midnight, he saw they had stopped. They'd dismounted to rest while deciding what to do. They had apparently decided the stream led nowhere they wanted to be. When they left, they headed due east. But before they did, at least one had laid with Jezebel, as evidenced by her still-moist and most odorous neckerchief. He shook his head and returned to the saddle, now convinced he would catch up to them by first light.

Dawn caught him passing through an outcrop of massive boulders. So did at least ten Sisseton Santee warriors, several of whom aimed rifles at his head. A few appeared on top of the boulders while the others blocked his way front and rear. Escape was impossible; reaching for the Colt, unthinkable. As he made the sign of peace and said *"Hau, mi kolas,"* several young boys scrambled on top of the boulders from behind them to look down at what their warrior brothers had caught. Fargo glanced among the young faces and smiled. They were being taught well.

An armed warrior motioned for him to dismount. He wondered if they had already denied him the pleasure of skinning the Bible Boys alive. He assumed they had, for he knew he was damn close to the gang of butchers. The ever-alert warriors would have easily spotted three riders.

The Indians quickly relieved him of the Colt and Sharps. They tied one end of a long rope to his wrists. He watched one of the warriors hoist a youngster up on the saddle and hand him the other end of the rope. The youngster was told to take in some of the slack and tie it to the horn. Fargo knew he would walk the rest of the way.

Leaving the boulders, they joined a hundred or more Sisseton Sioux moving west. No one stopped to come poke at him. They did, however, turn and stare at the white man. The Ovaro and Fargo were consigned to eat their dust at the rear of the long line of Nakotas.

By noon his mouth was drier than old cotton, his lips were parched. Worse, his raw throat burned for water. He was covered with dust from head to toe. When he stumbled and fell, the young rider neither looked back nor paused for him to get up. Hard earth, grass stubble, pebbles, and rocks big as his fist tore into his flesh as he was dragged along. Somehow his reserve strength and will to survive got Fargo back on his feet. This time he increased his pace and took up a coil of the rope's length so he'd have a few seconds to right himself if he fell again.

The big man agonized each time he saw the youngster drink from the canteen. He forced himself to look away when the boy sloshed some of the precious liquid on his face and head.

By sunset Fargo was nearly delirious, stumbling, staggering to stay up, to keep moving, wanting so badly to lie down, knowing that blissful moment would probably never come. With eyes closed to deny the cloud of dust a moist spot to collect on, his head bent so tired, on legs and feet that had long since become numb, Fargo trudged forward, determined to survive. He walked all night.

When he bumped into the Ovaro's powerful rump, he staggered back and collapsed. He opened his eyes to a morning sky and heard a drum's slow throaty beat. Smoke caressed his dust-filled nostrils. He smelled the aroma of meat cooking.

The youngster and four warriors stared down at him, the boy coiling the rope. Without thinking, Fargo spoke English when he gasped, "Water. Please, give me a drink."

One of the warriors understood enough of the white man's language to comprehend Fargo's plea. The man told his companions, "He wants water." All of them laughed, then jerked him to his feet and force-marched him among a sea of tepees and stopped at the entrance to one. There he was made to kneel and wait while one of the warriors went inside.

He overheard the subsequent conversation easy enough, although whoever the warrior conversed with spoke in a low voice. Fargo's problem was the Nakota dialect. He had trouble with it and the Dakota's. Where the Lakota, which he knew best, used the L the Dakota used the D and the Nakota the N. Regardless of how the word was spoken—Lakota, Dakota, or Nakota—it meant the same: allies.

The warrior reported, "We found a white man and brought him to you. He is outside. What do you want us to do with him?"

After a silence the other man said, "Take the prisoner

to Yellow Dog's tepee. Tell him I will come and we will discuss the matter."

Upon hearing Yellow Dog's name, Fargo decided not to speak in Lakota. Many years earlier, before he learned the Lakota dialect well enough to understand it and make reasonably clear conversation, the big medicine man and he had a run-in, and Sunka Zi lost. Fargo beat him senseless after the arrogant man falsely accused him of stealing an Indian pony. In fact, he was returning it after taking it from the idiot who stole the animal.

During the brawl incited by the medicine man, Fargo had called him Dog Shit. Not only was Yellow Dog a dangerous man, he had a remarkable memory. Under the circumstances, Fargo dreaded seeing the man again.

The warrior emerged through the tepee opening and gestured for the others to bring Fargo along. On the way to Yellow Dog's tepee they passed many cooking fires tended by women with their dogs nearby. But Fargo's eyes saw only the moist bags made from buffalo stomachs that hung from tripods, dripping, wasting the life-supporting water.

He'd never seen this many tepees before. There were hundreds, maybe thousands of them almost back to back for as far as he could see. He believed the entire Sioux Nation was present. The outside markings of the tepee the warriors led him to identified it as Sisseton and the dwelling of the medicine man. Numerous scalps dangled from the tops of the spiraled tepee poles. Fargo grimaced when a warrior stood beside the opening and called Yellow Dog out.

The medicine man's hard face appeared at the opening. His eyes flared when he recognized Fargo. Yellow Dog smiled as he withdrew inside and said, "You have done well, Many Scalps. Watch this white man closely. He is dangerous and a thief."

The warrior glanced to his three companions and nodded. They instantly closed tighter around their captive. The warrior told Yellow Dog, "Kills in Rocks instructed me to tell you he will come and discuss the white man with you."

Yellow Dog grunted. Fargo couldn't interpret the guttural sound. It could have meant approval or the equivalent of an "Aw, shit!" Knowing Yellow Dog, the latter was probable.

He listened to Yellow Dog's movements and assumed the man was dressing for the occasion. He also heard a sleepy female voice grumble for the medicine man to make less noise.

The constant slow beat of the unseen drum and the high-pitched shreeings of whistles made from eagle wing bones told the Trailsman the sun dancers were lined up and proceeding to the arena. He wondered which of the four days of dancing in the blistering sun this would complete and how damn thirsty the dancers were. He knew they received neither water nor food throughout the four-day sun dance. They too must be dying of thirst.

Yellow Dog stooped and came through the tepee door opening. Fargo watched his adversary as the dark redskin stood upright and studied him without expression or emotion. Yellow Dog had painted the left half of his face white and the right half soot-black. The eye surrounded by white seemed enormous while the one in the black appeared almost invisible. He wore a head covering fashioned from the head of a huge yellow-haired dog. The dog had been skinned, and its neck, back, legs, and tail hung down the medicine man's back.

The canine's long mouth was open and its lips drawn back tightly to bare its big teeth in a vicious snarl. The dog's eyeballs had long since been removed and the cavities painted dull red. Around the medicine man's neck hung two necklaces, one made of bear's claws and the other, a long loop of buckskin with a white buckskin bag tied at the bottom. He wore an apron made from what the Trailsman recognized as a black bear robe.

Tan knee-high buckskin leggings and Santee moccasins completed the ensemble. His left hand held a large gourd rattle and the right a feathered stick on the end of which were four eagle feet spread full open for seizing. Fargo wondered what was on the man's mind.

The one huge dark eye and the two red cavities above it looked at Fargo. The medicine man spoke Nakota. "White man, I never thought we would meet again. Before this day is over, I will eat your heart and feed your bowels to the dogs."

Fargo believed the man would damn sure try.

"Take the thief to my sweat lodge and strip him naked," Yellow Dog growled to the warriors. "Heat fifty stones."

Fargo's gut tightened, for he knew what was in store for him.

8

The lodge stood apart from the encampment, out in the open on parched land. Fargo stood helpless while one of the warriors removed his clothing. One stood by with his rifle cocked and ready to fire should the big man resist. The other two and several young boys stacked the fifty stones in a pyramid in the fire pit, then surrounded them with long pieces of dry pine. A wad of tinder was inserted in the conical arrangement and set on fire. Within minutes the bonfire roared, its flames licking high and warming the stone core.

Naked, Fargo sat watching the fire and rising sun and listening to the much faster tempo now beaten by the drummers. Like himself, the sun dancers had a long and terribly hot day in front of them.

He'd watched the stones become white-hot before Yellow Dog and Kills in Rocks approached, leading an entourage of warriors and elders. Without ado, they formed in a circle and sat to decide the Trailsman's fate. He was dragged to the center of the circle and made to sit facing Kills in Rocks and Yellow Dog, who sat on the headman's left. Kills in Rocks wore tan buckskin, neck to toe, and his graying long hair flowed free over his shoulders and down his chest and back. Though his face was wrinkled, it exuded an inner serenity mixed with a wisdom made possible by his many years of life. Fargo believed he would prove to be a fair man.

He looked into Kills in Rocks' eyes and muttered, "Water. I need water."

Kills in Rocks told a warrior to give him a sip. The warrior left the circle and returned with a buffalo horn filled with water and handed it to Fargo. The big man gulped the contents of the black horn dry and handed it back. "Thank you, *toonk-ah-she-lah*," he said to the old man.

Kills in Rocks made no indication whether he appreciated being called grandfather or whether it offended him. Neither did he question Fargo as to whether or not he spoke Nakota. Yellow Dog launched the discussion about what to do with the big man. He stated his position clearly when he grunted, "This man is a thief. He has also desecrated He Sapa. He must die."

The old man didn't comment for a long time. He stared into Fargo's lake-blue eyes, as though trying to see his soul, searching for a speck of something to justify not killing him as proposed by the medicine man. Finally he blinked, took a deep breath, and said, "Yes, you are correct, Yellow Dog. The white man must die, but not now, not until the sun dance is over and the sacred tree is down and taken away. Then you can kill him for what he has done."

Yellow Dog's body language conveyed his annoyance at the delay. After a moment of obvious thought, he spoke. "You will be obeyed, Kills in Rocks. I will not take his life until after, as you have said."

"Good," the old man said softly. Standing to leave, he glanced to the glowing stones and added, "Purify him for the journey."

After Kills in Rocks and his entourage departed the

site, Yellow Dog and his men formed a tighter circle around Fargo. The medicine man said, "You thought he was being compassionate. All Kills in Rocks did was prolong your pain, white man. Your suffering will begin when the stone people are so hot we can see through them. But that will be only the beginning. I have other sufferings for you while waiting for the sacred tree to come down. Don't sit there looking as though you don't understand. I know you speak Lakota. You know what we're saying."

"And when will that be?" Fargo asked.

"One more moon," the medicine man replied. "I say you will not see the new day." When Fargo flicked his eyes up, glanced to the departing entourage and then to the medicine man, Yellow Dog grunted the explanation, "No, I will not kill you. Nobody will. You will kill yourself. I say you will not be strong enough to survive the night." He rose and told a warrior to come get him when the stones were ready, then left.

For the next hour the sun baked down on Fargo's broad shoulders and back. He alternated gazing into the fire, at the now transparent stones, and at the collection of tepees that stretched literally from horizon to horizon. For the time being settlers moving westward were safer than they had ever been. But that condition would change shortly. Yellow Dog said the sun dance would be over tomorrow. That meant shortly before the sun went down.

By dark the tall cottonwood in the center of the dance arena would be down and carried away. Then they would begin the four days of feasting to celebrate the spiritual event. On the fifth day the allies would break camp and start journeying back to their designated hunting grounds, the Lakotas to the west of the Black Hills, the Dakota to the east all the way to the Missouri, and the Nakota to the east of the river and beyond as far as the Chippewa would allow. Then all hell would break loose.

Yellow Dog returned, interrupting his thoughts. The big medicine man immediately disrobed. He selected two warriors to sit in the circle inside the lodge, one on each side of Fargo, who would remain bound at the wrists. Completely naked, Yellow Dog crawled through the small dome-shaped structure's sparse entrance and sat just inside at its right edge, then beckoned for the two warriors to bring the captive inside. Fargo entered without resisting.

Inside the buffalo-hide-covered dome, they placed Fargo on the west, facing over the stone pit and through the opening at the east. One of the warriors sat on his immediate left and the other on his right. If anything went wrong once the flap came down over the opening and sealed them inside in total darkness, the warriors would shove the big man onto the searing stones and give Yellow Dog enough time to get out of the lodge.

The warrior tending the fire used elk antlers mounted on one end of a sturdy pine pole to bring the stones to the entrance and poke them inside. Yellow Dog guided the Indian-style pitchfork to the pit, then with deer antlers removed the stones and arranged them in the pit. By the time twenty of the stones were in place, everyone inside was sweating profusely. By the time the fiftieth stone was added to the pile, the heat was intolerable. They were all suffering, bent over and breathing slowly, eyes closed. One half of a black geode filled with water and containing the buffalo horn was handed inside and set just east of the stone pit.

The medicine man nodded to those outside. They lowered the door flap over the opening. The inside of the lodge instantly became pitch-black. With no place for it to escape now, unbridled heat built up just as instantly. Fargo dared open his eyes and stare into the hot glowing transparent mound of stones. I'll never again complain about the hot sun, he muttered to himself.

Yellow Dog said, "Hot enough for you, white man?"

When he poured the first of four hornfuls of water on the stones, the water exploded in sharp hissing spats and the steam hit the top of the dome and dissipated down along the hide coverings. Fargo held his breath, grimaced, and cringed as the steam cascaded down over his body. The warrior on his left yelped and Fargo heard him gasp for cooler air, his nose and mouth sucking close to the ground. Taking the warrior's lead, Fargo knelt, bent his face to the ground, and discovered the air was indeed much cooler though still very hot. Yellow Dog and the warriors began singing.

At intervals, the medicine man continued to pour water on the searing hot stones as he and the warriors sang to the spirits. Finally all three of them screamed, *"Me-tock-we-oh-seh!"* The flap flew up. Steam rolled out the opening. Fargo slowly drew his face from the hot wet soil and stared out the opening, gulped the unbelieveably cooler air. Both warriors lay faceup on the ground, their chests heaving as they too sucked in fresh air.

Yellow Dog, who sat by the opening, hence, got first relief from the sudden burst of outside air, looked across the pile of stones at the Trailsman and grunted, "Good. I don't want you to die in here, white man. This is but a small part of your suffering. The beginning." To the warrior standing outside he said, "Refill the bowl," and handed the geode to him.

Looking back to Fargo, he said, "That first round was nothing. The second will cook your brain, white man. This I can promise. If you last long enough for your turn to pray, then I suggest you beg the Great Spirit to let you die." The geode was handed inside and placed in position. Yellow Dog called for the flap to be lowered and secured.

Once again the inside of the lodge became totally dark. The damp air immediately turned hot, then searing, when Yellow Dog poured water from the horn. Fargo bent his face to the ground and suffered his back to take the heat while the medicine man and warriors sang to the spirits again. The wet air was so intensely hot that it was all Fargo could do to withstand it. His senses faded in and out and his mind swam in dizzy spells. Vaguely he heard them cease singing and the warrior on his right begin a prayer. A pebble struck the big man's shoulder and he heard Yellow Dog grunt for him to pray if he could.

Fargo sat erect and prayed, "Oh, *toonk-kah-she-lah*, hear my prayer. Give me the strength, Grandfather, to endure this pain. Have pity on me, Grandfather, and these men, my brothers, and our brothers who are dancing, praying to you out in their sacred circle. Grandfather, they are praying for you to let all the people live long lives, be healthy, and have good hunting. They are offering to you the most precious things they have, their flesh and blood, Grandfather. Hear their prayers, Grandfather, and ours. *Me-tock-we-oh-seh*."

Yellow Dog poured six hornfuls of water at the conclusion of Fargo's prayer. The big man shoved his face down into the muddy soil in search of relief in Maka Ina's belly. He heard not the other warrior's prayer and only some of the medicine man's. He listened to the water sizzle on the heap of stones. Clearly, the medicine man was being extremely cruel. Fargo called upon his strong inner resolve to sustain him and sat erect to take the full brunt of Yellow Dog's brutality.

Again the flap swung up and open. A dense cloud of steam rushed out through it. When the incoming fresh air diffused the heat and the air that carried it, the medicine man raised his eyes and saw Fargo sitting tall, smiling at him. Without preamble Yellow Dog dumped all the remaining water onto the stones, signaling a premature end to the sweat, then left the lodge. Once again the big man had beaten him.

Fargo crawled out of the sweat lodge after the warrior who sat on his left. As he stood, he saw Yellow Dog walking toward his tepee. The beaten man hadn't even bothered to dress. A boy chased along behind him with his garb cradled in both arms. Fargo sat with his back against the lodge and inhaled the fresh air—hot, of course, but dry.

After a few moments a warrior who had not gone inside the lodge came and motioned for Fargo to stand. The stocky fellow held a geode. It was not filled with water. It was filled with red liquid, made from ingredients unknown by Fargo.

The man called for two other men to come help. When they were in position to contain Fargo should he resist, the man with the geode dipped a finger into the red liquid and painted a sacrificial stripe from the top of Fargo's head down his spine. The red stripe went down both legs to the bottoms of his feet, up across his big toes and back up the front of his legs, before continuing up Fargo's abdomen, the length of his breastbone, up the neck, and into his beard at the chin. From there the stripe bisected the Trailsman's lips and nose, passed between his eyes, across his forehead, and met its beginning on top of his head.

The job completed, the warrior gestured for Fargo to sit. He glanced among the tepees and thought about Sings Loud Woman and the cowhand, Cyrus, whether or not she had gotten back to her people and was here now. If she is here, he considered, then she hasn't heard about me being caught by the Sisseton. Still too early for the word to get around.

Sings Loud Woman was in his mind when Yellow Dog returned to break the vision. Fargo glanced up and smiled, not to intentionally irritate him, but because the medicine man had gone to his tepee to smear a fresh layer of paint on his face. The medicine man shot him a hard look, then started walking toward the sound of the drum. He shouted to the warriors behind him, "Get rope. Bring the white thief."

Fargo rose and walked inside a box of warriors. Yellow Dog had taken long angry strides; he was now out of the big man's sight. His escorts, however, seemed to know where they were going. They wove through one group of tepees after another, always toward the drumbeat, which grew increasingly louder. Naked children paused in their play to watch the strange passage, while others ran inside their tepees and stared, frightened, through the opening. Women cast curious glances, but continued tending their fires with the big hunks of meat slowly broiling over them. Fargo's mouth watered from the delicious scent. He wondered if he would ever get to drink water again.

The steady fast drumbeat became even louder to the Trailsman's ears when his captors led him out of the vast encampment. They were but a stone's throw from the large sun-dance arena, which was surrounded by a shady arbor of pine branches. Under the arbor sat many people watching the sun dancers, who were disbursed around the circular arena. Each danced in tempo with the drumbeat while facing inward toward the tree.

Nobody seemed to notice the big naked man with the red stripe, at least Fargo didn't catch them at it. They skirted the north side of the arena for less than fifty yards and stopped under a towering ponderosa. Fargo thought,

So, this is their hanging tree. At least I'll be out of the scorching sun.

At the medicine man's feet lay two large sunbleached bull buffalo skulls. He stepped between them to Fargo and grunted, "You can smile, white man." He jabbed Fargo's muscled chest with the sharp eagle talons, shook his rattle in his face, and chanted incantations Fargo did not understand.

Finally, on signal from Yellow Dog, a warrior slashed Fargo's wrist bindings and removed them. Fargo massaged his aching wrists and cracked his big knuckles, then rubbed his muscular arms and shoulders while waiting for the noose. Yellow Dog told the man holding the coiled rope to pitch one end of it over the large tree limb he pointed the gourd rattle at.

Fargo watched the coil sail over the limb and snake down the other side. Then to his surprise, Yellow Dog had the warriors slam Fargo facedown on the ground and hold him there. He instantly knew why. One end of the rope tied his ankles together. He felt his feet leave the ground, then his legs, then his lower body.

He flattened his palms on the ground and pressed down in the nick of time to prevent his face from dragging across the hot earth as they hoisted him aloft. He dangled head down from the limb, his extended arms and hands a good six feet from the ground. He watched while long lengths of rawhide were tied around each of his wrists.

Yellow Dog stepped close to him and looked into his eyes and said, "White man, you are not smiling. Is that because all your blood is collecting in your skull?" Holding his hard gaze, he growled to his helpers, "Give this thief to the skulls."

Fargo watched them tie the free ends of the rawhide straps to a pair of buffalo skulls, then let them fall. As they stood back, the medicine man spoke again. "We will not kill you, white man. Our ancestors, the sacred buffalo will kill you for what you have done to the people and this sacred ground. We will leave you now so you can smile in private as you die." He turned and took several paces, halted, and added, "If you are alive when the sacred tree is taken down, this will be a sign from the spirits they have favored you for reasons of their own, and you will be set free."

The big man watched them disappear among the tepees. He began testing the wrist bindings and found it impossible to loosen them. Then he tested the bindings at his ankles by wrenching every which way, and found them tight as ever. After much twisting and trying everything he knew to make the ordeal less painful, he gave up and relaxed to conserve what little energy they hadn't sweated out of him.

He found he could ignore the pain from muscles stretched to the point of tearing if he focused attention on the sun dancers. From his upside-down position he watched the sun reach its zenith, then begin lowering. Several of the sun dancers danced to the cottonwood to kneel and grasp the trunk in prayer. The dancers went to the tree four times, and after the fourth trip they ran back to their positions in the sacred circle.

Each sun dancer, Fargo noted, was connected to the tree with a long thin rope. One end of it was tied high on the tree trunk, just below the Y formed by the two main branches. To the other end was tied a yoke having two ends.

Attached to each of the yoke's two ends was either a slim piece of chokecherry limb with one end whittled to a sharp point, or an eagle's foot with the sharp talons spread full open. Either way, talons or pins, they were inserted in the flesh above each of the sun dancer's chests, and this completed the connection.

At the last second of the final run, the sun dancers spun to face the tree, the connecting rope and yoke drew taut—the flesh above their breasts was pulled way out—then flesh and blood flew back toward the tree when their momentum tore the talons or chokecherry limb pins from their chests.

Fargo shook his head, not in disbelief, but at their strength and resolve. He told himself that if they could stay in constant movement under the blazing sun for four days without food or water, and give of their flesh and blood, then so could he.

Fargo continued to concentrate on the sun dance. The low angle of the sun told him the third day of dancing would soon end. Then, unlike him, the sun dancers would leave the arena and go purify themselves in the four sweat lodges to the west of the arena. After purification they would go inside the sun dancers' tepees, lie down, and go to sleep. "Lucky rascals," he mused aloud.

As he knew they would, the sun dancers left the arena when the drumming ceased. He watched the evening shadows lengthen, change into twilight, then into darkness. In his painful solitude he watched the sacred fire at the sweat lodges for a while, then glanced among the cooking fires he could see in the great encampment.

His muscles, his entire body, every cell, burned as though on fire. He could no longer flex any muscle, and it became impossible for him to continue ignoring the torture. Soon his body became numb, not that this gave him any relief from the excruciating pain, for the numbness tore at his brain and invaded his mind. With the cold feeling of imminent death came delirium. Abstract visions appeared in his mind. With them came abstract sounds.

Fargo saw himself standing nude among a sea of buffalo skulls, watching a mighty herd of stampeding bison thundering toward him. As the wall of shaggy hair and black horns was about to trample him, the charging herd vanished, instantly replaced by a stormy sea, with towering angry waves lashing at his face. He saw himself struggling in the water to keep from drowning. A beautiful Indian mermaid dressed in pure white buckskin held her hand out to him. Her whispered voice lilted in the wind's fury. It said, "Wake up, wake up. Open your eyes, big man."

He felt his eyelids flutter open, but he saw nothing. The wind racing in his brain went away, then so did the crashing of the waves in his ears. Now the silence was worse than the fury it relieved. The tender lilting voice spoke again. "Bull Buffalo-Prick Man, it is I, Sings Loud Woman. Look at me, big man."

He felt water splash on his face and instantly licked that which trickled over his lips. Cutting his eyes toward the ground, he saw her standing there with a bag of water in one hand and a scalping knife in the other. When their eyes met, he gasped, "Water. Give me a drink, please. So thirsty, so—"

"No," she interrupted, "not yet. After you are down. We must hurry, big man." She severed the rawhide straps, and the heavy skulls fell. With their sudden release came unmitigated pains that shot up both his arms and tore into his shoulders. He clenched his teeth, groaned until the torment subsided. "Take the knife," she whispered, "and cut the rope."

He grasped the knife's bone handle and strained, groaning, to bend at the waist. He forced his shoulders upward so the hand holding the knife could get at the rope, then sliced part way through it before collapsing to hang down again. "I'm exhausted," he told her. "Must catch my breath."

"Have strength, big man. Next time you will succeed."

He wondered. Taking a deep breath, he folded upward, grabbed his ankle with his free hand, and severed the rope. He hit hard on the ground and rolled onto his back, gasping. She instantly had the bag to his mouth. Fargo took big gulps of the cool water. She rubbed the drippings over his face, neck, and chest. Between gulps he asked, "How did you know I was here?"

She grinned, saying, "All the women are gossiping about the big white man who has a real big muscle with a red stripe painted on it." He saw her glance to his thighs.

Sitting up, he guzzled the water bag empty. Sighing, he said, "Thanks, Sings Loud Woman. Now, if you will show me where to find my horse and clothes, and my guns, I'll be on my way."

"Are you crazy, white man?" she gasped. "Your horse is with the Sissetons' ponies, guarded by their warriors. Your clothes and guns are in their medicine man's tepee. To get any of it is impossible. They would discover and kill you on sight. No, you must run into the forest and hide in the hills."

Fargo didn't intend to leave without his things. Holding the knife up, he said, "Take me to the pony guards first, then show me Yellow Dog's tepee."

"No," she insisted. "They will catch you and—"

He clamped a hand over her mouth. "Shhh. Don't worry, Sings Loud Woman. I can do it. I must. I can't walk into Gully Town naked and unarmed. They would laugh me out of the territory. Show me the way."

She stood, sighed, and looked beyond him. "All right, I will show you the way . . . after."

"After? After what?" He followed her gaze to the dim

shape of a huge boulder. "Why are you showing me a damn boulder, Sings Loud Woman? Is someone there?"

She stepped around him and headed for the stone. He watched her take several long strides before he hurried to catch up. The boulder was flat on top and about as high as a kitchen table. She raised the hem of the buckskin dress to her breasts, then sat on the flat surface with her legs draped over its edge. Her eyes fixed on his. No words were needed. None was uttered.

Fargo's rose to the occasion. He parted her legs and wedged between her hot thighs. She pressed her face against his chest and took his length in both hands and guided it in. He heard her gasp as he went in deep, then moan when he began the rhythmic assault. "Eeeyaaeeii," she whimpered through lips drawn tight over clenched teeth. "Faster, faster and deeper. Eeeyaaeeii . . . you are big." Her legs locked around his waist, her heels dug on his ass, urged him to plunge deeply.

He pulled her head back, brought his open mouth to hers; they kissed and fought with their tongues. He moved his hand to her hard butt and pulled her to him with each strong thrust. In his mouth her hot breath murmured, "Aaagh . . . aaagh, good. Oh, oh, oh . . . I'm bursting inside. More, big man, more . . . aaagh, eeeyaaeeii!"

When he exploded deep inside her, she locked her long legs around his waist and squeezed. "All of it," she whimpered. "Give it to me." He felt her inner seizures contracting and releasing, squeezing him dry. Only when he began to soften did she unlock her legs and release him.

Fargo turned his head. "We must go, Sings Loud Woman, before you take what little strength is left in me. To the pony guards first."

She led him around the western perimeter of the encampment, through trees and rocks, and stopped behind a stand of tall bushes. When she parted them, he saw many ponies tethered to makeshift hitching rails. The magnificent black-and-white Ovaro stood among them near the center. His saddle and other tack were together on the ground where two guards sat talking. Fargo whispered, "Take off your dress, then walk out where they can see you in the firelight. Make them notice you. When they do, beckon them to you, then lead them behind the bushes."

She glanced up at him. "What if they kill me? What if—"

His chuckle was low as he placed a hand over her mouth. "Sings Loud Woman, I promise killing you the normal way will be the last thought in their minds. Just do as I said."

He watched the dress come up over her head. Draping it on the bushes, she shook her head and began a protest. "I don't think this is such a good id—"

"Shut up," he hissed to cut her off. "Nothing will happen to you, only to them." He nudged her out from behind the bushes, then peered through them to watch the sentries' reaction.

She went part way unnoticed by them and stopped. Both Fargo and the two lithe warriors heard her when she began singing in a low tone. She nodded toward the bushes, then turned her back to the two, bent over, and patted her rump. After a thrilling pause the two young men rose and sprinted toward her. Sings Loud Woman giggled as she danced to behind the bushes. Fargo was nowhere in sight.

She stood with her slim legs parted and waited for them. Both came around the bushes in a dead run but halted when they saw her pose. Both young men stood close beside each other, facing her, their eyes lowered to her dark V. She watched Fargo emerge from the darkness and creep up behind the heavy-breathing pair. She stepped to the man on her left, curled an arm around his neck, and fondled the other fellow with her other hand. The scalping knife carved across the throat of the fellow she teased on. Moving quickly, Sings Loud Woman drew her arm away from the other man's neck to make room for the knife. Before the dead man dropped, the knife slashed his companion's throat.

Fargo said, "Get dressed, Sings Loud Woman, then follow me." He went to his saddle, picked it and the other tack up, and took all to the Ovaro. He was cinching on the saddle when Sings Loud Woman appeared. Fargo looked at her curiously. "Tell me," he said, "did anything happen between you and that kid, Cyrus, on the way up?"

She giggled. "If he wasn't falling off me, he was missing the place and stabbing it in the ground. I finally made him lie on his back, then got on him. Big man, it was his first time. He hollered and screamed I was killing him. Kept his eyes closed and made terrible faces. When it throbbed and started spurting, he groaned real loud and almost fainted. I was happy when we came across a group of Oglalas going to the sun dance."

"Any trouble from them?"

"No. I told them what happened, how you saved me from the wolves and buried Two Fawns and Pretty Water. They accepted Cyrus as a brother. He spent the night in a warrior's tepee. After the morning meal he left."

Patting the pinto's neck, Fargo said, "Now you can show me Yellow Dog's tepee."

"This won't be so easy," she told him, and glanced to the sky. "It would help if it rained."

He looked skyward and stiffened when he saw what she meant. The leading edge of storm clouds moving in from the west blotted out most of the stars. "Well, I'll be damned," he muttered. "When you least expect, there it is. Show me the medicine man's tepee."

Sings Loud Woman led him away from people outside their tepees and past those where it was safe. They were deep inside the encampment when she stopped and faced between two tepees and puckered her lips. Fargo followed her pucker and instantly recognized the backside of Yellow Dog's tepee by the markings on it. In her ear he whispered, "Look around these two tepees. See if it's safe for me to go to the medicine man's."

She did, returned, and whispered his path was clear.

Fargo kissed her for the last time and hugged her close. He whispered, "Good-bye, pretty woman. Thanks for all you've done. Now go before I weaken and carry you away with me. I do not want you around if anything goes wrong."

Her shoulders sagged as she looked into his eyes. When he saw her eyes begin to moisten and her chin tremble, he turned her away from him, patted her fanny, and sent her away. After she left, he clenched the knife handle in his teeth and dropped to his hands and knees to crawl to the tepee. He put an ear to the covering. Yellow Dog's loud raspy snoring rose and fell in an even rhythm.

Fargo pressed the cutting edge of the knife to the covering, waited for a snore, then made the first slit. Three snores later he completed the long vertical gash. Gripping the knife with his teeth, he gently pulled the long cut apart and looked in. Yellow Dog lay on his side, facing Fargo. That Fargo saw him alone represented a plus, for it meant he wouldn't have to kill the bitching woman he had heard when he first arrived. His clothes, gun belt, and weapons were neatly piled inside to the left of the front opening.

If I can get around him without awakening him, his thought began.

In that instant two things happened simultaneously.

Yellow Dog's eyes flew open. Fargo knew by the stunned expression that the big medicine man could not believe what his eyes were seeing.

And before either man could blink or make a move, four monstrous bolts of lightning struck tepees nearby, which caused them to explode.

Fargo dived through the opening as monumental thunder and lightning shook the ground. The medicine man caught the big red-striped man in his arms. The knife slipped from Fargo's teeth and fell onto the buffalo robes that covered the ground inside the darkened tepee. As they struggled to kill each other, a howling wind struck the encampment. With it came a torrential downpour. Yellow Dog's tepee caved in. Under the collapsed covering each had the other by the throat with one hand, searching over the robes for the knife with the other. Fargo found it first.

Pressing the sharp cutting edge to Yellow Dog's throat, he growled, "Good-bye, Yellow Dog. Have a long journey to the Spirit World." He sliced deep and wide.

When his hand holding the nape of the dead man's neck withdrew, it held the leather thong bearing Yellow Dog's medicine bag.

Fargo crawled beneath the covering to where he'd seen his things and found them in the downpour already coming inside. More lightning struck as he gathered the clothing and weapons in his arms. Thunder, mightier than before, roared across the encampment and vibrated the ground so much Fargo found it difficult to stand. He ran through the cold, wind-driven rain, skirting tepees, to the Ovaro. He mounted, clutching his gear to his chest, and hurried the pinto into the stormy night.

A group of warriors had seen him running among the tepees and gave chase. They leapt on ponies and charged after the big Ovaro, firing their rifles at the tall man astride it. Slugs whizzed past Fargo's ears. He urged the pinto into a fast gallop. As he rode east, he thanked God for the lightning that showed him the way and the downpour that shielded him from his pursuers.

After passing through a group of tall boulders, he wheeled the stallion to the left behind them and stopped. Bringing the Colt from its holster, he listened for the warriors, but they had apparently gave up the chase or gone the wrong way. He waited a long time.

Finally he dismounted and started pulling on his soggy clothes. As he stuck an arm in his shirt's sleeve, a brilliant flash of lightning lit up the area and he saw Yellow Dog's bulging medicine bag fall from the shirt to the muddy ground. He picked the thong and bag up and stuck it in his pocket, then put on his boots and hat. After attaching the Arkansas toothpick to his left calf, he buckled the gun belt to his waist. Another flash of lightning showed him a wild red berry bush. He made time to gorge himself with berries.

Returning to the saddle, he slid the Sharps into its case, put the Ovaro at a walk, and rode off into the gorgeous, blessed rainfall.

9

Fargo punched out of the eastern edge of the Black Hills at dawn. A drizzling rain fell from a sky overcast with dark low-hanging clouds. At most any other time, and under different circumstances, the steady drizzle would be an annoyance. He relished it now, however, for the rain both hid him from any eager Sioux warriors who might still be trying to find him and it quickly washed his tracks away.

Because he'd been here before, remembered landmarks, and no longer had to follow somebody else's wandering trail, he took shortcuts as he skirted down this side of the Black Hills. As a result, he crossed the river much sooner than expected. He angled the Ovaro toward the northern rim of the Badlands and made good time, arriving shortly after total darkness came.

Fargo dismounted to rest the big stallion and squatted on his heels. Staring into the night rain, he wondered if he should wait for dawn. The thought of a clear day and the ungodly moist heat it would surely bring returned him to the saddle. He pressed on.

Within the hour the slow rain ceased, replaced almost instantly by a stiff breeze that whipped across his back. Now he shivered as he let the Ovaro's night vision lead them out of certain trouble, if not disaster. While the loose soil had quickly absorbed the initial rainfall, it could soak up only so much before turning muddy and soggy. Water stood in some places, especially the lower spots that had been bone-dry previously. In other areas the water actually still flowed. Progress was slow but steady. He could trust the Ovaro.

Much later, when he believed the jagged crests of the arid line of hills were to his right, at about the location where the phenomena occurred, the wind strengthened. With it came a deep rumble of thunder far behind him. Soon brilliant bolts of lightning stabbed out of the rolling clouds and exploded on the crests. He took these as signs from the spirits who lived here that all was well, for the bolts could easily have fried him on the spot.

An hour later the trailing edge of the black clouds passed overhead. The moon was up, surrounded by what seemed to him extra-bright stars. The wind lessened, then died altogether. The moonlight offered him safer passageways. He quickened the pinto's pace.

He left the Badlands by first light; at midmorning he passed the meadow where he'd seen the porcupine, then shortly after noon, he reached the creek at the bottom of the hill where he'd seen Jezebel join her father and brother. There he dismounted and started a small cooking fire, then got the Sharps to hunt for something small to eat. He had no problem kicking up several rabbits. Two shots and he had bagged his meal.

While the rabbit cooked, Fargo made a small lean-to by the creek to shelter his bedroll. Then he shed his clothes and reclined in the creek to bathe and inspect his body. The rain had cleansed him of the abominable red stripe; not one speck of it remained. Nonetheless, he washed all over, then spread his clothing out in the sun to dry.

As he did, he turned his pant's pockets inside out. In one he found Yellow Dog's medicine bag. Fargo sat to open it. He dumped the contents into his left hand, and several things fell from the bag. Among the huge dog teeth and toenails gouged from paws were eight gold nuggets, the smallest about the size of Jezebel Hanks' big nipples.

Fargo stood, dropped everything except the nuggets, and looked toward the Black Hills. A frown formed on his face as he muttered, "Is it possible? This makes twice Sioux Indians possessed gold."

Fargo awakened to see a star-filled sky. He dressed, got the Ovaro ready to ride, mounted up, and rode south. About midnight he came out of the foothills and saw Gully Town. Light spilled out onto the street in front of the saloon. Approaching, he saw several horses hitched out front and heard Calvin tinkling away on the piano. He glanced toward Avis' home. It was as black and forbidding as the spinster's dress.

Fargo loose-reined the pinto next to the horse he recognized as Cyrus' mount. He went to stand at the saloon's swinging doors, prepared to see Avis and her naughty nieces.

Six cowhands stood with shot glasses before them on the long bar. Jud Mott stood behind it with a half-empty whiskey bottle in his hand. The females were nowhere in sight. When the group burst out in leg-slapping laughter, Fargo stepped inside. Mott saw him first. His laugh vanished in a gulp, instantly replaced by a shocked expression that permitted only gasped stutterings. "Uh, uh, Mr., uh, er—"

Fargo stopped him with a hard look and said, " 'Evening, gents."

Cyrus leaned out of the pack. His expression also

registered startlement in which Fargo detected the hint of a lie. "Howdy, Mr. Fargo," Cyrus croaked. "We been wondering what happened to you."

Fargo bellied up to the bar and scanned the immobile cowpunchers' faces. Mott collected his wits and poured him a glassful of his best bourbon. Fargo sipped from it, saying, "Glad to see you made it back safe and sound, Cyrus. Anything interesting happen on the way up?"

But it was Calvin who answered from the piano. "Cyrus, he had a gooood time, didn't you, Cyrus? What all he did to that Indian girl would make a man want to go steal one for hisself. Ain't that right, Cyrus? Cyrus says it's the best he ever had, and that includes them French tarts in Saint Joe. Go ahead, Cyrus, tell him how she begged and fought you for more."

The cowhand shrugged and mumbled, "Aw, warn't nothing to it really, Mr. Fargo."

"Damn," Fargo said, and swigged from the glass. "I would have thought she would be hotter than a depot stove. You sure there wasn't nothing to it?"

"Yeah," a lanky young cowpoke began. "You been holding out on us, Cyrus?"

Cyrus hitched up his pants and made a disgusted frown appear on his face, as though he preferred not to discuss the matter.

Fargo's sinister I-know-what-happened grin egged the kid to speak before he did. "Aw, hell, fellers, you know how it goes with young girls that never did it before. Mostly jest a bunch of screaming and hollering. Kept her eyes closed most of the time. Gritted her teeth a lot too. That sort of stuff." He looked to Fargo for support. Fargo saw a plea in the kid's eyes when he asked, "Ain't that right, Mr. Fargo? You been around."

Fargo nodded. Why not? he thought. Only me and the kid know he's lying. When he changed the subject, Cyrus visibly breathed easy. "I expected to find three females with fire roaring out between their thighs when I walked in." He looked at Mott, clearly conveying he didn't want to hear any bullshit.

Jud hastened to reply, "They're gone, Mr. Fargo. All three of 'em left two days ago."

"By themselves?" Fargo asked, concerned. "For where?" Again he looked at Mott for the answers.

"Well, sir," Jud began, "they're headed for Saint Louis. A wagon train of settlers came to Gully Town for supplies and some rest. They were going west—to Oregon if I recollect rightly—and got as far as somewhere in Wyoming. That's where they got attacked by a mob of Injuns. Killed all but one of the men, a real skinny guy they called Hiram something, he looked scared half to death to me. Then Indians raped all of the women right down to the twelve-year-olds. After that those folks said to hell with Oregon and turned back. Satisfied and the others went with them when they left here."

"Was Elmer Dugan and his woman with the wagon train?" Fargo asked, hopefully.

"No, sir," Jud answered. "We haven't seen hide or hair of them."

Fargo reasoned Dugan was either a day ahead or behind the wagons filled with women and children and one helpless man. If he and Little Feather were ahead of them, then the group might be all right. Dugan's wagon was notorious for breaking down. They would catch up to him and he'd look after them. On the other hand, Fargo had taken the reverend's silver. He had to honor that commission whether or not he or those three liked it. As he lifted the glass back to his lips, a worse thought raced to mind, one he could not ignore. He saw Buzzard's Gap and the black flesh-eating scavengers circling over it.

He emptied the glass, then looked down the line of faces. "I'm not one to close the damper on an evening of fun, gents, but I suggest everyone of you keep your guns loaded." When they frowned, obviously more than normally concerned, he explained, "There's good reason to expect Sioux. They chased me out of the hills and may still be following me best as they can.

"But they have two other better reasons to attack Gully Town, or any other town or wagon train. When I found Sings Loud Woman, I also found the mutilated bodies of two other young Indian women. Before that the Miniconju told me they would make a reprisal for what the Bible Boys did to them. I warned Elmer Dugan about it and he said he was closing shop and going to Saint Louis. Now I'm telling you men to follow Elmer's wisdom." He glanced at Mott's drawn face and said, "I'm going upstairs. Send up a big steak, some red-eye gravy, and a bottle of whiskey. See to it that I've got ample supplies in my saddlebags and that I'm not disturbed." Fargo didn't expect Mott to hang around to comply with his requests.

They watched him go before downing their drinks. Upon entering Dora's room he heard their fast departure. Fargo went to a window. A cool breeze billowed the thin curtains around him as he looked toward the darkened cabin among the trees. He thought of Dora, her sister, and their aunt, thought of why they left and whether they were safe. He glanced about the balcony, wondered where feisty Jezebel and her kin were tonight. "If they are alive," he mused aloud. Without thinking why, he lowered both windows to the point where nobody could come through without waking him. He sat on the edge of Dora's bed to pull off his boots. He found sleep quickly.

A moonless but starry sky greeted him four hours

later. Again Fargo took his clothes and weapons to the front porch to dress and strap on the gun belt. He did not hurry to the livery to get the Ovaro. After walking the horse to the end of the street, he spurred it into a faster gait and headed south for the east-west artery.

Dawn had broken by the time he came to the junction and turned east. As he did, he looked back toward Gully Town and saw clouds of black smoke. The Sioux, he muttered to himself. Will they be content with burning the white man's little town to the ground? I think not.

He nudged the pinto into a gallop.

The sun, mellowed by the cool breeze, comforted the big man. He considered the rolling Nebraska landscape that surrounded him and the pinto, a sea of tall prairie grass alive from the rain, and wished for higher ground. From the vantage point he imagined both he and the horse would be insignificant specks. He rode on in the waving grass.

At sunset he came to the river and got off the horse. He walked along the bank and found where the wagon train had forded. He counted eight sets of fresh ruts in the moist soil. The ninth, slightly older set, was carved deeper than the others. Returning to the Ovaro, he believed an early start would make it possible for him to catch up to the wagons by the next sunset. He hoped they didn't make it to Buzzard's Gap before he got to the wagons.

Fargo unsaddled the stallion, spread his bedroll on the bank, and slept.

He was up and had the horse saddled before first light. On the far bank he climbed up on the saddle and set the pinto at a gallop in the middle of the wagon wheel's tracks.

The sun at his back was a huge fiery orange-red semi-circle when he topped a low rise and saw the wagons parked by the pond in the meadow. Wisps of smoke from cooking fires foretold they were all right. As he came closer, he spotted Dugan's Owensboro among the other eight wagons strung out in a row. He wondered why the Irishman hadn't formed the parked wagons in a defensive circle. He cut his eyes toward Buzzard's Gap, which loomed big as life and as equally treacherous, mirroring the setting sun's hot color.

Fargo rode in unnoticed, listening to their gibbers and chuckles. He dismounted and hitched the pinto to the back of a wagon. They had congregated to eat around a fire by the pond. One woman carried a stew pot as she served them, one by one. Elmer was the center of attraction, doing all the talking.

"We'll be in Saint Louis before you know it," he claimed, "jest as soon as we get that damn wheel of mine fixed."

Fargo shook his head and walked to them, saying, "Dugan, why aren't these wagons arranged properly? This place could be crawling with Indians by morning."

"We don't need you to be giving us any of your stupid advice," Avis' hard voice replied, and Elmer stood.

"What Injuns?" Dugan asked, and glanced about as though expecting to see some.

"Or the Bible Boys," Fargo reminded. "They're out here somewhere, on the loose again." He sat and accepted the bowl of soup handed to him by the frail haggard-faced woman. "Thank you, ma'am."

Their silence told him they were considering what he said. As he supped, he counted eight women, including his three charges and Little Feather, two men—Hiram, who fit Mott's description of being frail and frightened, and Elmer—and four children—two boys and two girls, one of whom was big enough if not old enough to have caught the marauding Indians' attention. The boys looked as cowardly as Hiram. With the exception of Little Feather, Avis, and the two sisters, the other women had the hard faces carved that way only by visiting a living hell and not forgetting the experience.

Avis sneered, "Why did you follow us? We don't want any part of you."

Catherine and Dora looked down when he cut his eyes to them. "Reverend Hunnicutt paid me well to deliver you safe and sound. I honor my contracts. We head west at dawn."

"Like hell," Avis spat. "We're going to civilization, to St. Louis, with these good and decent folks. Aren't we, girls?"

Dora and Catherine grunted. Fargo looked at Elmer and said, "After we finish eating this delicious soup, you can help me put these wagons right for the attack."

"Attack?" one of the women gasped. She stopped eating to look about, then took to shaking so badly that both her bowl and spoon fell from her hands.

Avis was on her feet instantly and censured the big man as she rushed to calm the terrified woman. Squinting at Fargo, Avis hissed, "Now, see what you've done? Don't we have enough trouble as is without you adding to it with your fears? Sir, your very presence makes me want to vomit. The mere sight of you makes me ill." Fanning the distraught female's face with a hand, Avis said, "There now, Mrs. Hoaker, everything's going to be just fine. Take a deep breath and hold it." Fargo saw angry eyes cut at him as the aunt snapped, "You think and act like you're the cock of the walk."

Both Dora's and Catherine's eyes kicked up. He heard Dora's soft mutter, "He is." Catherine grinned. Her blush suggested she wasn't thinking about a rooster.

Fargo put his soup bowl and spoon in the wash bucket and nodded to Dugan, then went to the lead wagon. As he muscled it around into a new position, Elmer came to help. Pushing on the right front wheel, he asked, "How you want them put?"

"In a half-circle. Both ends hard at the pond. That way they will have to swim to get at us." He looked at Dugan and grinned. "Elmer, do you know how to swim?"

"Uh, uh. Not if the water's over my head."

While they worked, Dora moseyed over with her hands folded behind her, ostensibly to watch, but Fargo knew by the way she pooched her breasts out that she had devious thoughts. She waited until Elmer was out of earshot before she spoke. "Pretty night, isn't it, Skye . . . darling?"

"Lovely," he replied without looking. "You could say it's perfect for wild romance. Light refreshing breeze, plenty of stars, wide open spaces—no pun intended, ma'am—and me and thee."

"Hunh. Big man, did you just think that up, or did somebody else say it first?"

"Beats the shit out of me. That's what you wanted to hear, though. Right . . . *darling?*"

Dora spun angrily and put her back to him. Her hands turned into fists as she stalked away, muttering loud enough for him to hear, "You can go to hell and rot there, for all I care. I wouldn't have it if you served it up on a golden platter."

Dugan, sweating from head to toe, walked up in time to hear most of Dora's parting remarks. "What was that all about? She acts mad as hell."

Fargo grinned. "Nothing. She's got a soft itch that she wants me to scratch. Give me a hand. One more to go and we're through."

They had finished positioning Elmer's overloaded wagon in the center of the arrangement when Catherine strolled up and more or less assumed her sister's earlier stance.

Elmer looked at her, then at Fargo, and said he was going to see if Little Feather needed him for anything. When he left, Catherine leaned her back against the rear wagon wheel and said, "Romantic night, wouldn't you agree, big man . . . honey?"

He stepped to her, looked down at her upturned face, and opened the top four buttons of her light-brown dress. Reaching in, he teased her nipples and whispered, "Would you go fetch me a cool dipper of water . . . honey?"

Catherine's right palm struck fast as lightning and splatted on his left cheek. She jerked his hand out of her dress and left in a huff, muttering, "Get your own damn water. Try to be nice, and what do you get? Nothing!"

He watched her rolling rump for a second or two, then he went to the Ovaro and led it up the creek a ways and out of the immediate glow of the firelight. There he removed the saddle and harness and turned the horse to graze. Then Fargo unrolled the bedroll so he'd face the creek and shucked his clothes. Lying down, he listened to the murmur of those huddled by the fire. Avis was still barking as the big man closed his eyes.

A soft sound behind him flicked his eyes open. His right hand grasped the Colt and the thumb drew its hammer back slowly. When he heard the same soft sound again, he rolled left and swung the gun up at Catherine. Lowering the gun, he said, "Honey, if you don't learn anything else on this buggy ride, you better learn not to sneak up on a sleeping man, but come in making noise. Now, what do you want?" He looked toward the fire, saw everyone had left, apparently for bed.

"You," she murmured. "I need you."

He uncocked the Colt and put it within easy reach on the ground. Turning onto his stomach, he propped on an elbow and looked up into her wide eyes. They were filled with youthful anticipation. "What for?" he fenced, knowing the answer.

Catherine moved to stand at his waist. Her eyes caressed his body as she whispered, "Fulfillment. Dora told us what you two did that night in her room at the saloon. I can't get it off my mind. Maybe I can if—"

His touch on her silky smooth leg stopped her in midsentence. Rubbing the leg through her dress, he suggested, "Why don't you take that ugly dress off and come down here with me? Nobody will see."

Catherine's smile was about as fast as her hands and fingers. Within seconds he watched the dress come up over her dark honey-colored head and fall to the ground. She blushed as she pulled down her lace-bottom drawers and dropped them on the dress. She wore no brassiere. Her breasts were fuller than he imagined, stood high and as proud as the magnificent nipples surrounded by a small circle of soft-brown areolae. He wanted to feel them, to gorge himself with them.

She saw his pleasure and drew a palm over them and down her body, pausing at her belly to focus his attention on its soft roundness and the exciting dimple in its center, then she moved the hand to the honey-covered mound above the swollen entrance to her eager passageway and fondled the lips with a long middle finger. Fargo involuntarily wet his lips.

He pulled her down to straddle his muscled chest, took her full rounded ass in his hands, and drew her hungry moist lips to his. She moaned as though she had just found heaven.

In that instant Avis spoke. "Catherine, what are you doing? My God, child, you—"

Then she saw Fargo's undeniably powerful prong stabbing toward the Little Dipper and cut short the forming condemnation. Avis gasped, "I do not believe what my eyes are seeing."

Fargo's grip on Catherine's tense rump urged her to ignore the distracting woman and continue as though Avis wasn't standing there stuttering to find other words of denouncement and disbelief. Catherine rocked on as she said, "Go away, Auntie. Fargo's tongue and lips are a thousand times better than yours."

"Well, I never," Avis began. "I'll go straight to hell and burn forever in Satan's fires, but—"

She moved to stand where Fargo could see her come out of her clothes. She kept her widened eyes on the slippery movements of her niece's crotch, hiding Fargo's face from the nose down, while she quickly removed her dress and undergarments. He watched a most beautiful ass blossom full bloom when she released it from the tight corset. Avis' amply rounded cheeks curved gracefully from the bottom of her spine, grew nicely, and did not sag at the bottom, but tucked in. Fargo instantly wanted to feel her ass.

He moved his eyes up Avis' body and his tongue up her young niece's hot slippery slit, which squirmed continuously. Avis had a slim waist with an outer belly button below breasts that would easily overlap the inside of a champagne glass. Both areolae and the nipples were extra large, definitely ready and begging to be sucked on. While her dark pubic hair was sparse, he still liked what he saw when she spread her feet apart and teased him with her compact short opening she'd heretofore kept under wraps. She showed him a wicked smile, then stepped out of his sight.

Catherine moaned and giggled and rocked on as though fanning his lips with hers.

Avis mumbled excitedly, "How in the world does one

get on something this big? Mr. Fargo, now don't you hurt me."

He grunted, she squatted. The big man felt her take the throbbing, waiting elongated muscle of blood and hot flesh in her hands. She put his swollen peak in position for insertion at her very raw, hot, and still-innocent gateway to bliss and gulped down her fear.

Staring at her niece's crack Avis reached back and spread her buttock cheeks and knees as far apart as they would go. Moving very slowly, with absolute caution, Avis fed the crown into her tight wet-with-water inlet. She instantly groaned, "Oh, my God, my God, I'm being ruined." He felt her dare for another inch or so. "Oh," she yelped. "It's tearing me apart!"

"Dammit, Avis," Catherine scolded, "just shove down and stop bellyaching. That, or get up and go back to the wagon. You're breaking our concentration, isn't that right, Fargo, honey?"

He grunted, Avis shoved. Fargo felt like an oversized piston being forced into an undersized cylinder. He was inside virgin territory that was damn hard to stretch. Now that she had gotten past the initial hurt, Avis romped like there would be no tomorrow. Her moans and groans, grunts and whimpers were ceaseless and all were as filled with ecstasy as her belly was with hot muscled weight.

"What's happening in there?" she cried. "It's making me dizzy." Fargo knew. Avis was having multiple orgasms, wonderful feelings she never before had. "I see shooting stars. God, they're beautiful." She shoved down harder than before.

Dora's voice came as she walked out of the darkness. "Well, well, looky here," she mused. "Two on one. Avis, don't you hurt that beautiful big man. Hear me?" She moved to stand over Fargo's head with her bare feet apart. Dora wore nothing. She came ready to seduce.

Catherine warned, "You'll have to get in line, sweet sister, and take your turn. We got him first."

Dora glanced at Avis' enraptured face. The woman's eyes were closed tight as a banjo string and her thin lips stretched just as tightly over gritted teeth. In her obvious pain, Avis was loving every split second of the thrilling experience.

Avis shrieked, "What is that burning me up on the inside? What are you doing, Mr. Fargo, that's setting me on fire?"

"Dammit, Avis, stop whimpering," Dora said. "You should have thought about that before you got on it. Okay, little sister, your turn on the big man's pole. Make it snappy, though, and leave some for me."

Catherine reluctantly backed off and sat on Fargo's heaving chest. Showing a winning smile, she cooed, "Big man, you sure do know how to heat up a woman." She bent with her mouth open and kissed him passionately, as though she savored his lips, mouth, and tongue.

Dora pulled her off, saying, "Don't be a hog. Move down and let me have a crack at him."

Avis disimpaled herself. Standing, she sighed, "Sin is glorious. I'll never be the same again. Can't wait to head west. How long will it take, Mr. Fargo . . . *sweetheart*? Two wonderful months? A whole year, perhaps . . . if we don't hurry?"

As Catherine's lips slipped over his relaxed prow to suck it back to its known greatness, Dora settled down for a dual lip massage.

Avis said, "Hell, and I thought that damn handle was bigger and longer than a fence post. Where, oh, where will I ever find another man like you, Mr. Fargo?"

Both Catherine and Dora answered, "You won't."

The Little Dipper moved, and so did Catherine and her sister and Fargo's tired tongue. Avis sat cross-legged and watched her nieces teach her a lesson or two or three. Occasionally she would sigh, then look up at the stars and get all dreamy-eyed. As she had so aptly prophesied, her life would never be the same again.

Early morning, just before first light, found them curled against the big man and all sound asleep with most satisfied expressions on their peaceful faces, especially Avis.

She slept on her back with her legs spread wide so the cool night air could rake the glowing embers still burning in a tender place.

10

Fargo's eyes shot open. He remained motionless, listening, cut his eyes left and right, peered into the darkness in those directions, then lowered his gaze down his body and watched beyond his feet. Only Catherine's soft slow breathing punctured the otherwise total silence. And that silence bothered him. The abrupt cessation of the sounds of the night is what woke him, and he would not dismiss it as a wolf or coyote on the prowl.

Sliding a hand up his torso, he clamped his palm over Dora's mouth. She awoke instantly. Fear filled her taut body as Fargo whispered in her ear, "Don't move a muscle, don't make a sound. We have visitors. Be still and keep your eyes moving and your ears wide open while I tell the others."

He moved his hand to Catherine's lips and awakened her. At first she thought he wanted to make love again and she nibbled on the finger between her lips until he repeated what he told Dora. Now she bit her lips to help quell a forming whimper of absolute alarm. He turned slightly, ever so slowly, and slid his palm over Avis' mouth.

The spinster's eyes flew open. His pain was immediate and excruciating when she bit his finger. She grunted and tried to rise, but with help from Catherine he held her down and crammed four fingers into Avis' mouth. He whispered, "Goddammit, woman, quit struggling and be quiet. We're about to be attacked. Don't make a sound, not one peep, not even a gasp, when I take my hand out of your face." He withdrew the fingers, looked at her, and rubbed them to make the pain go away. He thought, Woman, every opening in your body is tight as church mouse's.

He brought their faces close to his and told them, "We have to get back to the wagons. Take your dresses if you wish, but it isn't necessary because the warriors will rip them off if they get to you. Actually your nakedness would distract some of them long enough for us to shoot them.

"We go in single file. Stay in a crouch and don't tarry getting there. Plaster your butts to the side of Dugan's wagon and keep quiet.

"Avis, you lead out. Catherine, you count to three, then go. Dora, you follow your sister. I'll cover the rear." When they looked at him and grinned, he added, "Pun intended, ladies. All three of you have watchable asses. Go, Avis."

Avis did not take her clothes when she left, sprinting in a low crouch. Neither did the other two. But Fargo got his and the weapons.

All three were pressed flat against the inner side of the wagon when he got there. Pulling on his pants and gun belt, he issued orders. "Wake everybody, children included, except Elmer and Little Feather. I'll rouse them. Avis, you and Catherine take the wagons on the left, Dora gets those to the right. Wake them like I woke you. Tell them to gather right here. Understand?" They nodded. "Then go."

He looked over the side of the Owensboro. Dugan's

grizzly face was buried in the crook of Little Feather's massive left shoulder. She was wide awake, looking straight into Fargo's eyes. "Sioux warriors," he whispered. "Don't know how many, but they're out there. My guess is they will hit us at dawn. Let Elmer sleep. The first shot will bring him to life." They exchanged slight nods. Fargo dropped to one knee and waited for the settlers. Elmer began snoring loud as a train's engine pulling a steep grade. Good, Fargo silently speculated. The warriors will think we are unaware.

Fargo held muster after the thirteen people arrived. "Get in a tight bunch so you can hear me." They crowded in. He scanned among the frightened faces and stopped on Hiram's. The man was shaking like a leaf. "Do you have a gun?" Fargo asked him. Hiram shook his head. To the others he said, "Hold out your weapons so I can see them." He counted three pistols and three rifles. All looked serviceable. He didn't know about the feminine hands holding them. I'll know soon enough, he told himself.

One of the women held a revolver in one hand and a rifle in the other. He asked which she preferred. She clutched the rifle to her bosom. Fargo had her hand the revolver to Avis. Then he handed his Sharps to Dora.

"Okay, ladies," he sighed, "here's how we do it. Dora, you defend from that end wagon." He pointed to it and continued. "I'll be at the wagon on the other end, where I think we'll see them first."

He looked among the others. "All of you ladies except Catherine get bellydown under a different wagon. Hiram, you stay right here with the children till it's over. Once it starts, all of you can scream your heads off, if that will make you feel any better. Just aim and fire and keep doing it. We can't kill them if you don't shoot. And I believe all of you know what that means. Yes, ladies, we're playing a death game. Your choice on living or dying."

His serious gaze moved to Catherine. "You're our lookout. Stay at this wagon and watch for any who might be foolish enough to swim the pond. If you see one coming, yell, 'Pond.' Got it?"

Catherine nodded.

"That's it," he said. "Go to your positions. Good hunting. I'll shake your hands when it's over." Fargo left first.

From his position he alternated scanning the tall prairie grasses in front of the semicircle of wagons and checking the dawn, which was trying to break on the far side of Buzzard's Gap in the near distance. He wondered why these Indians hadn't taken a position at Buzzard's Gap rather than make a fight of it out here in the open. It didn't make any sense, but the fact remained the warriors chose the latter, obviously for reasons of their own. Staring into the dimly lit grass swaying gently in the light breeze, he wished the rain hadn't fallen on this place and perked up the green. Dawn broke slowly.

An arrow whizzed in. Its point buried in a board on the far side of the wagon where Fargo stood. As he aimed to fire, he heard Catherine yell "Pond!"

Then all hell broke loose.

At least six warriors burst from the grass and ran in screaming war cries. Fargo's bullets knocked two backward. Their companions swerved left, forcing Fargo to expose himself to effect a clear shot. As he swung with them, he heard the Sharps belch, then again. Elmer fired as fast as his woman could reload. Fargo shot two more painted Indians, heard Catherine scream, "Pond! Pond! Seven in the pond!"

The Indians screamed. Catherine screamed. The people under the wagons screamed. Hiram's shrill voice screamed loudest of all. The women fought for their lives. Warriors fell, staggered to their feet, and fell again. Catherine started picking up rocks and throwing them at the swimmers. One from her barrage of stones hit an Indian in the head. He sank below the surface, bubbles of death marking the spot.

Fargo caught a warrior crawling under the end wagon. He pulled the war-painted man out and sliced his throat with the Arkansas toothpick.

Dora swung around and shot a swimmer as he came onto the bank, then turned in time to ward off an attacker and blow a second belly button in his gut.

Fargo ducked behind his wagon and leveled the Colt on the swimmers emerging from the pond. He fired and left four lying on the bank before the Colt snapped empty.

Avis, or one of the other women at her perimeter, gunned down the last swimmer as he was about to power his hatchet into Catherine.

While hurriedly reloading the Colt, Fargo glanced down the curve of wagons. Dora gut-shot an Indian point-blank, then scooted under the wagon to reload.

Fargo saw Hiram and one of the youngsters sprawled on the ground. Several arrows protruded from their bodies. Fargo cursed under his breath, then swung and fired as a warrior came over the side of the wagon. The dead man fell hard onto the ground at Fargo's feet. "How we doing, Elmer?" he hollered. "Need my help?"

"Hell, no," Elmer's whiskey voice shouted back. "Me an' the little woman, we're doing okay."

Fargo climbed up into the wagon and stood to pick off redskins who were now inside the curvature. When the Colt's hammer fell on empty brass, he holstered it and drew his knife. The big man leapt to the ground and began stalking prey to stab. An Indian wielding a long deadly hatchet buried it in a woman's back, then rose and confronted the Trailsman.

Fargo grinned as he returned the knife to its calf sheath, then he spread his arms and began feinting the woman killer for an opening. They moved clockwise in a circle, sized each other up, then lunged at the same time. Fargo knocked his opponent's arms open and went for the throat. The two fell and rolled on the ground. Fargo ignored the fists pounding on his back and applied constant pressure. He watched the warrior's tongue stick out, heard his dying gasp, saw the eyeballs protrude. He flung the dead man aside and stood.

It was over.

Dora applauded.

Fargo glanced about the bodies, red and white, that littered the ground. Blood was everywhere. Gunsmoke hung heavy in the air. A blazing hot morning sun beamed down on all of it. Fargo called everyone out for muster.

He counted five dead whites—Hiram, one boy, and three women—and three walking wounded—one of the women and her daughter, and Dora. Dora's upper left arm showed a thin red ribbon where a knife had cut. The other woman had been beaten in the face. Blood seeped from her nostrils, and her badly split lips were a red mess. But her terror had pulled the trigger and blown the maniac off her. The girl caught an arrow on the outside of her right thigh. She broke off the fletched end then shoved the shaft on through. "I'll be all right," she said.

Fargo tousled her mop of red hair. "Hey, up there?" he shouted. "You and Little Feather still alive?"

Elmer's unconcerned face rose up out of the wagon. "Fit as a fiddle. Wanna chase 'em down an' get their scalps? They'll fetch ten apiece in Saint Louis."

Fargo chuckled. "No. Let them go. We need to bury our dead and be on our way. Avis, you and Catherine put some clothes on and look for a few somethings to dig a grave with."

"How about me, big man?" Dora asked.

Fargo looked at her and shrugged. "Get up in the wagon and be our lookout." He went to where the creek fed the pond, crossed over it, and walked among the trees to find a shady final resting spot. With a stick he drew a long rectangle in the loose soil. "We'll bury them here," he shouted across the pond. "Elmer, start dragging."

"What about the Indians?" the wounded girl asked.

The Trailsman looked at Buzzard's Gap. "The buzzards can have them . . . or the wolves. We'd be here all day if we bothered with them. I said this was a deadly game. Rotting in the hot sun is their penalty for not winning. Bring me a tool to dig with."

Fargo dug, Dugan dragged bodies. When they were all arranged in the bottom of the grave, Fargo deferred to Avis to commit their souls to God. She spoke eloquently and without once referring to Scripture. She concluded with a simple "Ashes to ashes and dust to dust." Tossing in a handful of soil, Avis added, "Amen." Fargo and Elmer put their shovels to work.

An hour later the two men replaced the broken wheel on Dugan's wagon with one from another Owensboro. Then they hitched his mules to it and teams to the other three selected for the journey. The other five they left behind and trailed the remaining horses behind their wagons.

Fargo studied Buzzard's Gap while he rode alongside the Conestoga commandeered by his three charges. Finally he spoke his mind. "I can't stop you from going to St. Louis. All of you are full grown, plenty capable of making up your own mind. You're free to make the choice. If you continue, I'll see that the reverend gets his money back along with a note explaining things. Incidentally, Dora, are you ever going to put clothes on again?"

"Gosh, big man, I dunno. You see anything wrong with me being buck-naked way the hell out here? Ain't nobody around to see me but my kinfolk . . . and you, big darling. Anybody ever tell you you're a handsome brute? And I do mean *brute*!"

He noticed Avis' lovely bottom tense, betraying her recollection of her near demise. "Once or twice," he answered. "Head for the slot—ooops! No pun intended this time, ladies. I'll ride ahead and check out the far side." He nudged the Ovaro into a faster gait.

Watching him ride ahead, Catherine said, "I don't know about you two shameless hussies, but I'm not letting that beautiful body get away. I want some more of him. A whole lot more, and I do mean *whole*."

Avis snorted. "Child, where's your mind? Mr. Fargo has more than you can handle. Why, he'd reduce you to mush on the inside in a week's time."

Dora sighed, "Sister's mind is below her waist. She wants the same things that drew me to the saloon. I'd dearly love to get reduced to mush . . . by him, that is."

"Not me," Avis replied firmly. "Ever since last night I'm having trouble just walking without feeling shooting pains. I'm going to find me one about this long and big around." She parted her palms about six inches, then curled a finger to touch the thumb.

Dora and Catherine exchanged doubtful peeks out the corner of their eyes.

Fargo approached Buzzard's Gap cautiously. He watched the many buzzards roosting on the pinnacles for early-warning signs of impending danger. If just one bird moved, he would turn and race back to stop the wagons. But none did, and he rode through the gap. On the other side he searched all directions with his keen eyesight to spot the slightest movement that would give away an ambush.

He saw nothing but heat waves rising from the landscape. He rode halfway to the mammoth boulder before halting and scanning all its surfaces, then turned back, convinced the pathway was clear. He dismounted in the gap and waited for the wagons.

Dugan arrived first. The women driving two of the wagons followed close behind him, Avis and the sisters after them. Fargo watched Avis' team enter the gap as he told Dugan they had nothing to worry about. "Didn't see a thing on the other side," he said.

Elmer snapped the reins and said, "Giddyup, fool mules."

In that instant a rifle barked. All of the buzzards promptly took to wing, rose as a swirling dark shadow of death. The wounded girl sitting beside her mother in the wagon immediately in front of Avis' screamed, "Help me! Help!" and tumbled from the seat to the ground.

In rapid succession two more shots rang out. Dugan's two lead mules fell dying.

Fargo's eyes swept both peaks as he drew the Colt. "Everybody on the ground," he shouted. "Get down on the right side of your wagons!" He ran, hugging the wall of the gap to the left of the wagons. Passing Avis, he shouted, "One's high left, the other high right. Keep that son of a bitch on your side eating gravel. I'm going up after his friend."

Dugan fired at the same time both of the ambushers did. Fargo glimpsed rock shatter high left. Now the women blasted away. Slugs chewed into rock and whined off into the heat. Fargo cleared the gap and began working his way up the rocky side facing the meadow and pond. Only the circling buzzards were safe.

Above him he heard the ambusher's rifle barking louder as he climbed over the rocks and went higher, his eyes fixed on the spot where the gunman was hiding. Then he saw the glint from a sun ray kissing off the rifle barrel when it was moved. He found a solid toehold and pushed downward. His head and eyes came above the hot surface of a jagged rock near the summit.

Fargo's eyes met Noah Hanks'. Noah fell back, pulling the trigger. Two bullets screamed past the big man's chiseled face. Fargo's shots found Noah's left eye, then his heart when he twisted sideways. Fargo yelled down to the others, "It's the Bible Boys! Keep that bastard pinned down till I get at him!" He looked across the gap to find him, saw nothing but rock, and began descending. He'd made it to the bottom and was crossing the gap when Dugan's rifle coughed twice. A Bible Boy toppled from his cover near the peak and fell screaming. His body met the hot ground and the dull thud of flesh colliding with an immovable solid object spawned a mushroom of dust. The gap fell silent.

"Everybody stay put," Fargo warned. "There's one more up there somewhere." As he scanned the peaks to spot Jezebel, he wondered where they'd hidden their horses, how he failed to see them.

He squinted toward the boulder and saw only it gleaming under the sun. He was turning to tell the women they did well when out of the corner of his eye he saw the big dun with Jezebel bent low in the saddle explode from behind the boulder and ride hard for the eastern horizon. Fargo ran to the Ovaro and leapt in the saddle, spurred the pinto, and went after her.

The dun was fast, almost as fast as the big black-and-white stallion. Fargo was gaining, but slowly when he saw them. Four mounted Omaha warriors riding straight for the dun. He reined back and halted. "They can have her," he muttered under his breath. Jezebel Hanks deserved what the Omaha would give her before putting her out of her misery. He turned around and headed back to the wagons, confident of her bleak destiny.

What he found at the wagons wasn't pretty. In addition to the dead girl, there were three other dead. The girl's mother lay crumpled on the ground next to her. Her dark-brown hair was matted with blood and brains. And both of the young boys lay sprawled in puddles of muddy blood. As they stood surveying their dead, they heard gunshots, soft puffs, for the sounds came from distance, dampened by the shimmering heat.

The woman from the wagon behind Dugan's screamed and clutched her little girl to her bosom. A terrible fear filled both mother and daughter's eyes, and their faces were drawn and twisted grotesquely.

Dora muttered, "Mrs. Davidson's gone mad, Fargo. She's been going that way since Wyoming."

Fargo sighed heavily, for that was all he could do. "Put her and the girl in your wagon for the time being. Looks like we're stuck here for a while, till those Omahas make up their minds what they want to do next, try us or go home with one white man's scalp." He looked at Elmer, grimaced, and said, "A rotten day, my friend. Let's clear the gap and bury the dead. Maybe it will rain tomorrow."

By sundown they had the gap cleared of the wagons and Avis had said appropriate words about the departed for the second time this day. Hers was a reflective mood as they huddled around a small fire and laid plans for the morrow. Dugan didn't feel well. He loved those two mules more than even Little Feather realized. Catherine handed Fargo a tin plate of beans, then moved to Dugan and did the same. Avis and Dora stared into the fire. Neither wanted food. Little Feather shook her head when Catherine offered her a plate.

Fargo ate half his beans before speaking. "I'll ride half a day with you tomorrow, then turn back and wave good-bye."

Avis, still gazing into the fire, mumbled, "Good riddance. Ever since you rode into Gully Town there's been nothing but bloodshed. Mr. Fargo, trouble is your companion. Wherever you goes, it goes."

Catherine thought for a moment, then spoke softly. "There's nothing I want in St. Louis. I want to see Mama and Daddy."

Dora, still naked as ever, looked at her but said nothing.

Fargo ate the rest of his beans. Around the last mouthful he said, "Elmer knows the way. He'll see that you make it there." Standing, he told Catherine it was time to go to bed and warned her they needed a good night's sleep.

"I'll be along in a minute," she answered. "This being my last night and all with my sister and aunt, I want—"

"No problem," he interrupted, nodded, and walked away.

He lay fully dressed on the bedroll spread wide in the gap, taking benefit of the breeze resulting from the vortex effect. He found it easy to shut down his mind and close his eyes for sleep. Two shots snapped them open and brought him to his feet. Dora's and the mad woman's screams drew the Colt. Fargo hugged the gap's north wall with the Colt ready for action as he hurried toward the fire. He saw Avis and Catherine writhing on the ground, Avis about to roll into the fire. He peered into the night as he rushed to pull the spinster back. As he tugged her away, he glanced at Catherine. The bullet had entered her left cheek and come out on the other side.

During the glance, Jezebel stepped from the darkness, aiming her pistols at the big man's heart. Smiling, she said, "Well, big feller, I tole you I'd be back. Hope you didn't think them four scrawny Injuns'd tear me up. Anyhow, now I got me two more good reasons to blow your balls off—Pa an' Mark. I ain't gonna lay with you thi—"

That's as far as she got. The Sharps roared. A red hole appeared in her forehead. Jezebel Hanks fell backward, dead before she hit the ground.

Dora stepped from behind Dugan's wagon. A wisp of smoke curled out of the Sharps' barrel. Little Feather said, "Fargo, the preacher woman is not dead."

He knelt and cradled Avis' upper body and head to his chest. As he brushed a strand of hair from her face, he glanced at the blood soaking her dress at the chest. She smiled and whispered, "I didn't mean all the hard things I said to you. Don't know why I said them. Just an angry woman I guess. I—"

"No, Avis," he cut in, "don't talk. I'll—"

"Dammit," she interrupted in a stronger voice, "can't you see I'm dying? I have to make things straight . . . proper before I go." She gasped, gulped, then choked out, "Thank you, Mr. Fargo for . . . last . . . night . . ." Avis' eyes closed and her body fell limp in Fargo's arms and against his chest.

He looked up at Dora and said, "Go get blankets and wrap your sister in one. I'll hold your aunt awhile longer." The Trailsman looked west and east, wondering which had the greater pull and why. No logical answer came to him, only the mystery of people wanting. Exactly what, not even they could explain fully or adequately. But they would die in the quest.

Avis and her niece were laid to rest side by side in a grave dug next to the one containing the settlers Fargo had buried earlier. He asked Dora if she would say something over them. She shook her head as tears formed in her eyes, but finally whispered, "Good-bye."

Fargo looked at Little Feather and Elmer. They shook their heads and remained silent. The crazed woman and her daughter sang "*Shall We Gather at the River*" far off-key but with sincerity and firm belief. Then Fargo shoveled.

Seventeen people in nine wagons had congregated by the peaceful pond a little more than twenty-four hours earlier. On this side of treacherous Buzzard's Gap, only six in two wagons now gathered. As he said he would, Fargo led them across the rolling Nebraska landscape until the white ball of fire blazed overhead. He moved up by the Irishman's wagon, reached in, and shook his hand, saying, "Buy that pretty woman of yours a brand-new dress and a fancy wide-brim hat when you get to Saint Louis. Take care, Elmer Dugan. You too, Little Feather." Fargo touched the brim of his hat, then turned to bid Dora farewell.

She stood with her feet apart and her hands on her hips, waiting for him. He came alongside her and stopped, leaned back in the saddle, held the reins high, and nodded.

Dora stretched a leg high and extended a hand. He gripped it, then her ass as he yanked her from the ground to him on the saddle.

Snuggling his bunch-up into her crack, she looked over her shoulder and said, "Big man, I will show you many times on our way to San Francisco why they call me Satisfied."

He looked through Buzzard's Gap and wondered if the Reverend James Hunnicutt and his spouse realized how much hell he was bringing to them.

RIDING THE WESTERN TRAIL

☐ **THE TRAILSMAN #90: MESABI HUNTDOWN by Jon Sharpe.** Skye Fargo finds himself with a woman whose past includes a fortune in silver buried in a lost mine somewhere in the trackless Mesabi range ... but she can't remember where. The Trailsman must jog her memory while dealing death to the killers who want him underground—not in a mineshaft—but a grave. (160118—$2.95)

☐ **THE TRAILSMAN #91: CAVE OF DEATH by Jon Sharpe.** An old friend's death has Skye Fargo tracking an ancient Spanish treasure map looking for a golden fortune that's worth its weight in blood. What the map doesn't include is an Indian tribe lusting for scalps and a bunch of white raiders kill-crazy with greed.... (160711—$2.95)

☐ **THE TRAILSMAN #92: DEATH'S CARAVAN by Jon Sharpe.** Gold and glory waited for Skye Fargo if he could make it to Denver with a wagon train of cargo. But first he had to deal with waves of Indian warriors who had turned the plains into a sea of blood. (161114—$2.95)

☐ **THE TRAILSMAN #93: THE TEXAS TRAIN by Jon Sharpe.** Skye Fargo goes full throttle to derail a plot to steamroll the Lone Star State but finds himself with an enticing ice maiden on his hands, a jealous spitfire on his back, and a Mexican army at his heels. Unless he thought fast and shot even faster, Texas would have a new master and he'd have an unmarked grave. (161548—$2.95)

☐ **THE TRAILSMAN #96: BUZZARD'S GAP by Jon Sharpe.** Skye Fargo figured he'd have to earn his pay sheparding two beautiful sisters through a Nebraska wasteland swarming with scalphunting Indians ... but it looked like nothing but gunplay ahead as he also rode upon a clan of twisted killers and rapists called the Bible Boys that were on the hunt for bloody booty and perverse pleasure. (163389—$3.50)

Buy them at your local

bookstore or use coupon

on next page for ordering.